Ms. Menon is a wife and a mother of twins. She has an educational background and a career in finance. Even when her life was circling behind numbers, she had always been fascinated and obsessed with books. She has published children's books. She started writing stories for children after the twins entered her life. She loves spending time with her family. Her family and books are the most precious assets for her.

Experiencing grief in life can either make you or break you. Like anyone else, I was going through a dark phase of my life, with my mom fighting cancer and not being able to travel and be by her side due to COVID restrictions. The pandemic made me realize the value of relationships. The material things seemed useless. My whole life, I have supported my mom and been her strength in every little aspect. But when she needed me the most, all I could do was to helplessly stay in my country and watch her fight her battle alone. She is a fighter. She bravely succeeded in her battle in killing the cancer cells. Her boldness and courage gave me the strength to pursue my dream of becoming a published author. So I decided to surprise my mom with this book. I would like to dedicate this book to my brave mother.

J C Menon

THE INTERTWINED FAMILY

AUSTIN MACAULEY PUBLISHERS®

LONDON • CAMBRIDGE • NEW YORK • SHARJAH

ISBN – 9789948756170 – (Paperback)
ISBN – 9789948756187 – (E-Book)

Application Number: MC-10-01-1106279
Age Classification: 17+

The age group that matches the content of the books has been classified according to the age classification system issued by the UAE Media Council.

Printer Name: iPrint Global Ltd
Printer Address: Witchford, England

First Published 2024
AUSTIN MACAULEY PUBLISHERS FZE
Sharjah Publishing City
P.O Box [519201]
Sharjah, UAE
www.austinmacauley.ae
+971 655 95 202

Writing a book is like fitting all the puzzle pieces in the right way to embark on the perfect picture. In my journey of becoming an author, the strongest puzzle piece was my husband, without whom I would have never experienced this beautiful chapter of my life. I love him so much for putting up with all my craziness and being my strongest pillar.

One

A loud thunderclap jolted me up from my deep sleep. For a moment, I couldn't recollect where I was. And suddenly, I was shaken by the sound of my phone ringing. I picked it up immediately, as I knew calls at this time of the night will only be for emergencies.

"Hello!" I said.

"Hello Dr. Jennifer, Mrs. Paul is in labor. She is crying out of pain. Please, come ASAP," said the worried nurse.

"Did you check her vitals? Has the cervix dilated?" I asked.

"Yes, ma'am, her vitals are stable, and the cervix has dilated up to 8cm. The contractions are closer too," the nurse reported.

"OK, I will be there soon," I replied and hung up.

I got up from my bed, freshened, and changed my clothes. It's a regular practice to have a fresh set of clothes ready, as I get called for emergencies. Without wasting time, I took the elevator and went downstairs to the hospital. I live in the same hospital building. It's a 24/7 working hospital with an in-patient facility. The doctors, who would be called up for emergency and critical conditions, are accommodated in the same building. The doctor's consultation rooms and patient wards are up to 10 floors, and the rest five floors are apartments for the head nurses and doctors. I'm Dr. Jennifer, a specialist OB-GYN Surgeon practicing at the City hospital, one of the best hospitals. I was chosen by the hospital for my incredible academic performance and my special quality to handle a crisis birth situation using minimal resources. I work at the city hospital for five days a week, and for the remaining two days, I have made a practice to visit the nearby town to provide free consultations and check-ups to the underprivileged. The satisfaction and contentment I get by serving the needful, who are deprived of proper medical facilities are indescribable. If given a chance, I would happily serve them my whole life. But, I have bills to pay and fulfill my own necessities and essentials to live.

As I reached the labor room, my patient, Mrs. Paul, was going through painful contractions. After examining her, I informed the couple that we will have to wait for a little while for the cervix to be dilated up to 10 cm. I explained to Mrs. Paul that her contractions will come up more frequently, but until the cervix opens up fully, we cannot take the baby out. It was her 2nd child, so she already knew the drill, but it was my responsibility to explain the process.

We were busy for the next 4-5 hours. It was completely exhausting, but everything vanishes the moment the precious bundle of joy enters the world. The pure site of bliss and joy on the mother's face and a mixture of pride and emotion of the father is worth every ounce of effort we put in through the process.

While giving a glimpse of the baby to the parents, I proudly announced, "Congratulation! It's a girl!"

It was already 3 am when everything was done, and Mrs. Paul was moved to her room.

The nurse asked, "Are you going back home?"

I said, "Since I'm up, I might as well complete some of the pending paperwork. I will be in my cabin. You can reach me if anything."

"Shall I get your coffee to the cabin?" she asked.

"No, Lexi, thank you. I shall get it myself," I replied.

I went to my room, and on my way, took a cup of coffee from one of the machines in the hospital corridor. My cabin was modestly arranged with a good taste of comfort and privacy. There was a window opening up for plenty of sunlight to fall, which had a view of the city streets. It was pouring heavily outside. When I entered the room, the pitted-patter of the rain on my window was loud. Outside, it was dark, and not many people were seen on the road below, as it was the middle of the night and raining heavily too. The splattering rain, the soaked up roads, and the dimming lights of the city and a baby girl born on a stormy night like this evoked a huge wave of emotion and memory in me. The memory I want to forget and the memory that I can never forget.

The Past

Two

On contrary to how Mrs. Paul wrapped her baby in her arms trying to protect her from the storm outside, some years back – thirty years back to be more specific – on a similar rainy night, I was born and abandoned. My birth parents didn't even try to keep me safe on a dangerous night; instead, they left me in a cradle outside a child care center. I don't know anything about my birth or my birth parents. All I know is that I was abandoned in front of our orphanage in the middle of the night by someone. I was left out in the cradle, which was placed in the front yard right under the big sculpture of Jesus Christ. In the sculpture, Jesus has spread his arms wide open, gesturing warmth, protection, and love. So, maybe, whoever dumped me might have thought Jesus would protect the baby.

Mother Catherine was the head of the child care center. She has a warm, nurturing presence. Her eyes, soft and kind, hold a depth of understanding and compassion. She often wears simple, practical clothing usually a modest dress with an apron that allows her to move freely as she tends to the children and the needs of the orphanage. Her hair, streaked with a few strands of grey is usually pulled back into a tidy bun, though a few loose strands frame her gently face. She carries herself with a calm and steady demeanor, her posture upright and confident, exuding an air of reliability and strength. Her hands, though marked with the signs of constant work, are gentle and reassuring, always ready to offer comfort and support. Mother Felicia who was second to Mother Catherine, on the other hand had a vibrant and energetic presence. She has bright, expressive eyes that sparkle with enthusiasm and a genuine affection for the children. She favors casual yet practical attire, like jeans and a comfortable blouse which allow her to engage actively with the children and participate in various activities around the orphanage. Her complexion is fresh with a natural glow that reflects her energy and dedication. She moves with a lively grace, her steps are quick and purposeful, embodying a sense of youthful vigor and a readiness to take on any task that comes her way. They both together ran the center successfully. They are two exceptionally loving and caring, selfless people that I have ever known. Ironically, the child care center was named "The Family". They intended for the children to feel at home and view the other habitants as their family members. The children who lived in The Family weren't all orphans. All of them had parents. Parents who weren't in a position to take care of their children like underprivileged people, single parents, sick parents, and various other reasons. I was the first and the only child who was abandoned within a day of birth with unknown parents. That made me the odd one and the special one at the same time.

Like any other night, Mother Catherine was in her room getting ready to go to bed. She had a regular practice of offering prayers before sleep. While praying, she doubted she heard a cry. The thunder and rain were so loud that she couldn't be quite sure of what exactly she heard. She wondered what could that be. Then she continued to pray. But subconsciously, she is a mother, a mother to so many children. And so her mother's instinct started kicking in. Her heart raised; she felt sick in her stomach and could barely focus on her prayer. She heard the cry again. It was more like a squeak. She apprehended something terribly wrong. So decided to go outside and check for herself. She asked Mother Felicia to join her. They took a torch and went to the front yard. As they were getting closer, the cry was painfully audible. They feared to see what they thought they heard. It was evident by now that it was the cry of a baby. And from the squealing and screeching sound, the mothers knew it was an infant. They walked in silence, picturing the terrifying ruthless act of someone abandoning an infant on a dangerously stormy night like this. They picked up their pace and reached near the cradle as quickly as they could. They lit up the torch and saw the baby.

"Oh dear Lord! This is a tiny baby. Looks like a day or two old," exclaimed Mother Felicia shockingly.

Mother Catherine quickly picked me up, and they went inside. They tried to calm me down, but I wouldn't stop crying. They covered me up with some blankets. Mother Catherine asked Mother Felicia to get Alex, the house nurse.

Alex was the in-house nurse who had a soothing and composed nature, emanating a sense of calm and reassurance. She had the most attentive and empathetic eyes, always observing and ready to respond to the needs of the children. she often wears her hair neatly pulled back into a ponytail, however since she was half asleep her hair looked messy with half of her hair out of the scrunch. Her face reflects both kindness and professionalism with a gentle smile that can put even the most anxious child at ease. Her overall appearance and nature create an aura of safety and trust, making her a beloved figure in the orphanage.

By the time Alex and Mother Felicia arrived, Mother Catherine fed me some milk. I gulped the milk in one go. Once my tummy was full, I looked peaceful.

Alex examined me and checked my temperature.

She said, "The baby looks fine for now. Let's wait until tomorrow to see if the temperature raises or any other signs to be worried about. Since she was out in the wind, there is a danger of infection or chest conjunction. But she looks fine for now. Will monitor her for the rest of the night."

Mother Catherine said with confidence, "I'm sure she is going to be just fine. She is a fighter."

Alex kept checking me at regular intervals throughout the night. Until the next morning, I was fine and took my feeds at the appropriate times.

Alex asked, "So are we going to keep the baby here?"

Mother Catherine replied, "There are certain formalities for that. At first, I will report the incident to the nearest police station and then confer with our head office at the same time and inform the child care, social service people, too."

"Until we have more information about the baby, we will not tell anything to the children here."

"Yes, Mother, I understand. You go peacefully, carry on with the legal procedures; in the meantime, Mother Felicia and I will look after the baby."

For the rest of the day, Mother Catherine was occupied with the paperwork and the formalities. She returned to the Family in the evening and told Mother Felicia and Alex that as per the police, there hasn't been any missing infant being reported yet. So, they have asked us to keep the baby until they have more information about it. The social worker will be paying a visit tomorrow to see the baby. And the head office also authorized us to look after the baby until we get any information from the police. Mother Catherine sneaked near the bed and saw me sleeping peacefully.

She asked, "How was she during the day?"

Mother Felicia replied, "Oh, she is an angel. She took her feeds and slept the whole day. Poor thing, I can't believe someone could be so cruel."

"Let's not judge anyone without knowing the whole story. Everything happens for a reason and probably abandoning this little angel also has a heartwarming reason," replied Mother Catherine.

"But Mother, how are we going to handle the rest of the children? The baby cries from time to time, and it would be impossible for us to hide the baby for too long from the kids!" said Alex worriedly.

"Yes, you are right. But for now, we have to prioritize this baby's safety. She needs to be kept away from people and the outside world, as she is delicate and prone to infections. She will be safe in my room. Let her stay here. Once the word gets out, the kids would want to visit her which is not an appropriate action for now. Let's wait for the police reports, then we shall decide," said Mother Catherine.

The next day, the social worker visited me. She asked Alex about my health status and enquired a few other stuff. She then took all the details from Mother about my abandonment, and how they found me. She took a note of every information she collected from Mother and Alex. Finally, she said, "We will be conducting an investigation about the incident from our side too. And we will get in touch with you the moment we receive anything. But until then, the baby looks safe in your house. If you wish, you can keep her here or if there are any issues with you taking care of the baby, then we shall take her and put her up for adoption if no one claims her."

Mother Catherine wasn't ready to give me up. So she told the social worker that she would wait for the response from the police department and take a decision.

For the next couple of days, the Mothers and Alex had a tough time, keeping me a secret from the other children. The children had so many questions about the crying from their mother's room and Alex's sneaky behavior. Finally, Mother Catherine received a call from the police station saying that they haven't received any missing reports yet, and there hasn't been any inquiry about the infant. They added that they have recorded the baby as an inhabitant of the Family for now and that Mother can decide what to do with the baby. They also demanded that the mother had legally informed them regarding any decision she takes about the baby.

Mother Catherine and Mother Felicia discussed with each other what to do with the baby. They had two options, either they could keep the baby and let her grow along with the other children, or they could hand her over to the social worker. After a long hour of discussion, Mother Catherine said firmly, "I'm not yet ready to part ways with this little angel."

"Neither am I!" said Mother Felicia.

Then we should keep her. She was left in our door steps for a reason. Maybe she was given to us by Lord. We will give her all the love and care as per our capacity. Let her grow up with the other children. Maybe she might have a bright future from here.

"Since now, it's final that we are keeping her; let's give her a name," said Mother Felicia.

"What do you think is an apt name for her?" she asked.

"We should name her Jennifer. Jennifer means white fairy. She came into our lives on a dark cloudy night like a flash of thunder, emerging as a wave of emotion. She flew around our thoughts like a fairy and gently but firmly landed in our hearts. So I am sure the name Jennifer will do all justice to her," confirmed Mother Catherine.

"What an apt name you have chosen for her Mother," said Mother Felicia.

"I have another suggestion too," continued Mother Catherine.

"Jennifer is the only child in our Center who doesn't have parents. All the other children have a surname by birth. So I would like to name her Jennifer Family. The Family will be her family home, and we will be her family members."

"That is a noble thought, Mother. Even though she was abandoned, I feel that is a blessing in disguise for this little one," added mother Felicia astounded.

Mother Catherine took me in her arms and whispered my name in my ears.

Later when Alex visited mother Catherine, she told Alex about the name they had chosen. Alex loved it too. Alex asked how they would introduce me to the rest of the habitants. The children had a regular practice of gathering in the prayer room every evening. That time was called the sharing time. The children would share about their day or they could share about any new ideas they have or even just chit-chat with each other.

The basic idea of sharing time was to keep them connected. It also helped the introvert and shy kids to come out of their shells and express whatever they wanted. Mother Catherine decided to introduce me to the kids during that time. She thought the children will be in a chatty mood, so she could explain to them about my arrival to the family, and they could clear all the queries they would have.

"That will be the right time. I'm sure they will have so many questions when they see this tiny baby!" exclaimed Alex.

In the evening, all the children gathered in the prayer room as usual. Mother Felicia assisted them with their routine prayer and some instructions that she wanted to bring to their notice. Once that session was over, the kids automatically sat in a circle to share their views. But Mother Felicia said, "Hold on kids, today Mother Catherine wants to make an announcement. After you hear her out, we shall move to our sharing time."

As Mother Catherine walked in, the children diverted their focus to her.

Mother Catherine announced in a stern loud voice:

"How are you all doing my children? Hope all of you had an eventful day! Anyway! I think what I'm about to tell you might make your day even more eventful and memorable. A couple of days back, a new special guest arrived in "The Family". This new guest was uninvited, but her arrival brought joy and delight, so it felt like she was God-sent. I am sure you all remember the stormy night we had experienced a couple of days back! On that very night, someone abandoned a baby in front of our door steps."

Mother Catherine paused for a few seconds, giving time for the kids to sink into what they just heard. Even though the children were silent, their thoughts of inconceivable shock were deafening. All eyes stared at mother without a blink. She then continued…

"Even though it was dangerously blustery with heavy turbulence, this baby fought for her life like a warrior and survived the storm. We conducted an inquiry about her family with the help of the police but ended with no luck. So I have decided to make her one of us. She is the new habitant of the family. She is your new friend. There is something that I want all of you to keep in mind, she doesn't have parents unlike you. You all were brought here by your parents for various reasons. She came here as a destiny. So, be kind and gentle with her. Take good care of her. She is the youngest of all. I know all my children hold a golden heart, and you will love her truly. Please, welcome Jennifer Family."

As Mother Catherine made her announcement, Mother Felicia brought me into the room. There was a loud gasp and then pin drop silence. The children were struck with shock. They were perplexed by the vision of such a tiny baby and the thought of the merciless act of someone who had abandoned this helpless baby on a scary night. Mother Felicia walked closer to the children. None of them dared to come closer or touch me. I was peacefully sleeping in the safe hands of Mother Felicia. And unexpectedly, I moved my arms and legs and cooed, which made all the children dramatically react awwww! One by one, they came closer. One of them leniently touched me with their finger, making sure I don't break by the touch. Within no time, I was surrounded by numerous expressive looks. It was a blend of love, kindness, pity, sympathy, empathy, and shock.

One kid said, "She is so tiny."

Another one said, "Her fingers are like french fries."

Another one asked, "Why is she sleeping? Can we wake her up?"

Karen said, "I want to carry her. She is mine."

Karen was a five-year-old girl who had been living in The Family for two years. Her mother had schizophrenia. One time, she was sitting on the roadside with Karen, and Karen walked directly into the streets, and her mother completely ignored her. Her mother forgets and gets hallucinated frequently. A kindhearted passerby, who witnessed the incident, realized this mother is dangerous to this little girl. So he brought both of them to The Family. Mother Catherine took responsibility for Karen and sent her mother to the health care center, where she is being treated.

"What did you say, honey?" asked Mother Felicia.

"She is mine. She is my little sister. I love her. She is delicate and beautiful as a flower," Karen replied.

The mothers looked at each other. They have heard about soul connections and their intimacy. They thought if a kid is experiencing this kind of intimacy towards someone on the first look then this definitely was a thicker bond.

Karen caressed me and held on to my fingers. The love Mother Catherine saw in Karen's eyes for me assured her that we will have a bond for life and that we will love and protect each other. She thought when God takes away someone's family, he makes sure he sends someone who would have a deeper connection than family by blood.

From the first meeting, Karen became my best friend.

Three

Days and months passed by. From a fragile little living being, I began flourishing into a stronger active baby. I sleep less and have started smiling too. My arms and legs are stronger and chubbier. I have started developing my senses of recognizing people, smell, uniqueness in each touch, and taste of semi-solid food. Each individual smells different. Mother Catherine, Mother Felicia, and Alex trigger the sensation of warmth and security. Every time they come to me, I felt protected and happy. All the inhabitants of the family loved me immensely. The sound of the footsteps of the children and their playful cheers and screams generated curiosity and mischievousness in me. Visiting me and playing with me has become a regular practice for the children. Every day, I had cheerful visitors coming in and entertaining me. They all loved me and took good care of me. I was the center of attention in the Family. Alex made sure my health was top-notch. Mother Catherine and Mother Felicia pampered me. I don't know if it was fortunate or unfortunate that I was surrounded by so many warm and loving people. Gradually, the inhabitants of the family were turning into my real family.

Nonetheless, the whole pile of love and affection of all, combined, does not stand a chance against the love and bond of Karen. Karen visited me a lot. She would spend a lot of time with me. We play, she sings songs, which sounded really funny to me, but I cherished those moments. She was also a humongous chatter box. She kept blabbering something or the other. Even though I didn't understand a word, she said I admired her talks. Some days Karen would insist to sleep with me. She would create a massive fuss about it. But Mother Catherine wouldn't allow it. She said every child has to follow the in-house rules and sleep in their own allocated bed. Karen was my most favorite person.

The word of a newborn being abandoned in the child care house spread like fire in the town. There were a variety of reactions from the residents. For some residents, it was a preposterous act of viciousness to ditch a newborn. For others, it was a cowardly move by irresponsible parents. Some were empathetic and wanted to extend a hand of help. So they contacted Mother Catherine and asked what they could do to help. As per Mother Catherine's instructions, the residents donated plenty of baby food and baby products. Residents expressed their willingness to visit me. Mother Catherine scrutinized the visitors and allowed only a few to see me.

Because of some kind-hearted people, I have many toys, clothes, and a pram to roam around. Since the time we received a pram, I got a ride in our front yard every evening. The adorable drama queen of our home, Karen, persisted in taking me out for a ride one day. Mother Catherine had some concerns, as she was busy with some paperwork and couldn't join us. So she requested Alex to accompany Karen and me. Karen was excited to push my pram, and I had an enjoyable time with her. We were having a blast together. Alex rejoiced in our little playtime. Due to overjoy, Karen pushed me hard, and my wheels turned faster and tumbled over a rock, which threw me over. I fell hard on the ground, hurting my knee and lips. I began crying in agony. My knee and lips were bleeding. Watching me cry in pain broke Karen's heart, and she went into a phase of shock; she couldn't move an inch. Alex hurriedly picked me up and pulled Karen, and went inside. Alex examined me and was relieved to realize that there were no serious injuries. Those were just some scratches that needed a couple of band-aids. But Karen was the one who needed more attention, as the regret of pushing me was weighing hard on her. By that time, I had stopped crying. Alex tried to console Karen and said it was just an accident. But Karen was still in shock. Alex called Mother Catherine to talk to Karen.

Mother Catherine said, "Karen honey! Relax, it was just an accident. Yes, I agree that we should be more careful, but you didn't do anything purposely. It's OK, sweetie. Go and be with Jen. She will be delighted to see you."

Karen tightly hugged Mother Catherine and wept.

With a cracked voice and tears rolling down her cheeks, Karen said, "Jen is in pain. I threw her off the pram. She might not want to play with me anymore. She will hate me."

Mother Catherine lovingly replied, "No honey, that's not how relationships and bonds work. Trust me; she will be as joyous to play with you as she was before."

"You can try it yourself. Just go to her," convinced Alex.

Karen slowly came closer to me. I smiled at her; Karen was overjoyed to see my smile. She spent the rest of the evening by my side. Mother Catherine had a real tough time sending her back to her room. Finally, she somehow left, and we all fell asleep. Karen woke up early in the morning before all the other children and came running to mother Catherine's room to check on me. Mother gave Karen permission to be with me for the whole day. Karen spent the next couple of days completely taking care of me and being around me throughout. That accident made us inseparably close to each other. Mother Catherine and Mother Felicia were more than happy to let us bond, as they felt we could become each other's strength as we grow.

Time flew by, and I was ready to go to nursery. Since we didn't have money for school fees, we studied in our child care house itself. Few teachers who found immense gratification in giving free education to underprivileged kids came to our Center to teach us. I started my education like that. I had turned five, and Karen was 10. I was an enthusiastic learner. So my teacher liked me a lot. We all sat in the same room to study even though we were all of different age groups, but we had the same teachers. In the class also, I preferred being with Karen. Karen was good in my studies, and she helped me with my studies too. We literally grew together in every sense.

Karen was not an orphan. She used to live with her mother. But her mother was so poor that she couldn't provide Karen with any basic necessities. Karen's mother had some kind of mental illness too, which made her forget things. When Karen was a baby, she left Karen on the side of the road and completely forgot about her, and walked away. A passer-by, who witnessed this, called her back and reminded her of Karen. When the empathetic stranger studied the situation, he brought both mother and daughter to The family and narrated to Mother Catherine about the situation. Mother Catherine took responsibility for Karen and admitted Karen's mom to a mental health care center, where at least, she will be safe under a secured roof and will get food and care. There are days when Karen's mom feels absolutely normal. During those days, she would make a call to the family and talk to Karen. And then there are other days when she wouldn't even recognize her own room.

During holidays, the children of the family are allowed to live with their parents if the parents came and picked them up. Karen usually doesn't go anywhere, as her mom is in the health care center. But this time, Karen's mom expressed her desperation in spending some time with her daughter, so the health center staff allowed her to bring Karen to the Center and stay with her mom for a week. When Karen came to know about the plan she was extremely sad as she didn't want to leave me. Mother Catherine explained to her that she needed to spend some quality time with her mother too. And that her mother is sick and her presence will help her improve her health. Karen agreed for the sake of her mother. She came and hugged me tightly and burst out into tears. Then she left with the staff who had come to pick her up. I watched her go with a clinch in my stomach and a heaviness in my heart. But I didn't have a choice but to let her go. The only thing that kept me going was that she will be back after a week. Little did we know that it was a turning point in our life.

All the kids had left for the holidays. I was the only kid left in the family during that holiday season. It was during that time mother Catherine got all the maintenance work done in the building. There were workers working around the center. One of the workers found me cute and adorable. He inquired about me to mother Felicia. She enlightened him about my entry into the family and that I had nowhere to go. The man felt sorry for me. He became sympathetic. The next day, he came along another man and lady to the family. He insisted on meeting mother Catherine. Mother Catherine invited them to her office.

Ben, the worker, introduced the man and the lady to mother Catherine.

He said, "Mother, this is Stanley and Merideth. They live in the town nearby. I had gone to their house for some plumping job, and that's how I know them."

Stanley was tall and well-groomed, with a touch of silver in his hair that gave him a distinguished yet warm appearance. He wore tailored suit which enhanced his personality. His eyes, though reflecting his success, carry a hint of sorrow, a deep longing for the family he and his wife have dreamed of.

Merideth was elegant and graceful with a natural beauty that shines through even in simple polka dot dress that she donned. She wore minimal jewelry that complemented her sophisticated yet unpretentious style. She wore a simple pearl necklace a silver watch and her diamond wedding ring. Her hair was styled in soft waves and her gentle smile was tinged with a trace of sadness.

Despite their sorrow at not being able to conceive, their love for each other was evident in their supportive gestures and the way they held hands and exchanged comforting glances. As they prepare to adopt a baby girl, their excitement and hopefulness begin to shine through, bringing a new light to their eyes and a renewed sense of purpose to their lives.

"Hello, Mr. Stanley and Ms. Merideth, it's nice to meet you. Please, have your seat," said Mother Catherine politely.

All three of them took their seats.

"How can I help you, sir?" asked Mother.

"Mother, God has been generous to us in many ways. We both are working, and we make good enough money. We have a nice home and a good living. But God isn't generous enough to give us a child," said Stanley in a low tone.

"I have been wanting to be a mother for so many years. I have been craving for the presence and joy fullness of a child in our life for so long," said Merideth, sobbing.

Stanley comforted Merideth by holding her hand as she was sobbing in pain.

Stanley continued, "Yesterday, Ben told us about a girl child in your center who has no one. We would like to adopt her. We are willing to go through all the proper procedures and channels to proceed. What do you say, Mother?"

Even though the thought of being separated from me saddened my mother, she thought it would be good for my future. I will have a home and parents to Love and be loved. After giving it some thought, Mother Catherine turned to Stanley and Merideth.

Mother said, "You seem like nice people. Jennifer will be lucky to have you as her parents. But there are certain procedures and formalities for these things. I have to inform our higher authorities."

Stanley and Merideth were listening to each and every word coming out of Mother's mouth with immense hope in their eyes.

Mother continued, "I will need to see your identification details, both of your work details, annual income, and some more papers for verification. Once the authorities approve the papers, our social worker will come to you for a house visit. Once they also approve, then only you will get the child."

"Yes, Mother, we understand. We will provide you with all the details tomorrow itself," said Stanley enthusiastically.

Merideth blabbered something nervously.

Mother asked, "What is it? You can talk to me about anything. Do you have any concerns?"

Ms. Merideth?

Merideth passes a nervous glance at Stanley and said, "Are we allowed to meet Jennifer?"

"Of course, why not!" replied Mother Catherine.

Those words of the mother left Stanley and Merideth into a trance. The room felt quiet, save for the soft hum of a distant air conditioner. The couple sat still; their hands tightly clasped together. Stanley's grip was firm, a silent promise of support, which Merideth's fingers trembled with a mix of anxiety and anticipation. The room was adorned with cheerful, childlike drawings, but their hearts felt the weight of a moment that had been years in the making.

A door at the far end of the room opened slowly, Mother Felicia stepped in, holding my hand. I was a girl with curly hair and wide, curious eyes. I had worn a simple pink dress, my tiny shoes made soft tapping sounds on the floor. Merideth gasped, her free hand flying to her mouth as teers welled up in her eyes. Stanley squeezed her hand even tighter, his own eyes glistening with emotion.

"This is Jennifer," Mother Catherine said gently guiding me to move forward.

I looked up at Stanley and Merideth with a mix of shyness and wonder. Merideth couldn't hold back any longer. Teers streamed down her face as she knelt to my level, her voice breaking as she spoke.

"Hi, Jennifer," she whispered, her voice full of love and tenderness. "we have been waiting so long to meet you."

I hesitated for a moment, then stepped forward and wrapped my small arms around Merideth's neck. This was a totally unexpected reaction from my side which surprised everyone in the room. The contact broke something open inside Merideth and she began to sob softly, cradling me in her arms as if I were the most precious thing in the world.

Stanley knelt beside us and as he gently placed a hand on my back and said in a thick voice filled with emotion, "Welcome to our family, sweetheart."

Mother Catherine and Felicia were also overwhelmed with the whole scene. They were happy to see how comfortable I was with Merideth. Merideth and Stanley spent some time walking around and playing with me and then left. After watching how easily I bonded with them, Mother Catherine genuinely thought that things should work out for all and everyone be happy.

The next day, Stanley submitted all the papers Mother had asked for. Mother Catherine followed the procedure with extensive care, as she didn't want to make any mistake in choosing a family for me. By the end of the day, everything turned positive. There was nothing untrue about what Stanley and Merideth told about themselves. Within the next two days, the social worker also came back with a positive result. Now that all the paperwork has been done, and the verification about the couple was also favorable, it's time for mother Catherine to finally decide. That night, while I was playing in the corner of the room with my toys, the Mothers and Alex were having a discussion.

Mother Catherine said, "It feels like yesterday we got her from the cradle. A tiny little fragile thing."

"Ohh God, I remember the storm that night. She survived that scary night like a pro," said Mother Felicia.

"I'm worried about Karen. When she comes back, she is going to be devastated if she wouldn't find Jen," said Alex, concerned.

"Yes, I was thinking the same. But we have to make her understand that it's for Jennifer's good that we had to make a decision like this. It will take time, but I'm sure she will eventually understand. After all, she loves her Jen too much," conferred Mother Catherine.

"So it's decided. We are letting our little Jen go to her new family," said Mother Catherine with tears in her eyes.

Alex immediately came running towards me and hugged and kissed me. Mother Felicia also got emotional and rocked and loved me for a while and left. Mother Catherine hugged me tight the whole night while we slept.

The next day, first thing in the morning, Mother Catherine called up Stanley and gave him the happy news. He excitedly replied, "I and my wife will come around 10 am to pick up Jennifer."

I discerned that something unusual was happening. The mothers seemed overwhelmed. They made me wear a new pretty dress and caressed me throughout. As Mother Catherine was dressing me up, she explained to me the actual reason behind Stanley and Merideth's visit to our Family. She also added that she had decided to send me along with them and that they were loving and affectionate people. She assured me that they would take extremely good care of me. The assertiveness in Mother's voice made me realize that she had already decided about my future. If there was anyone I trusted the most on this planet, it was Mother Catherine, and I knew she would do the best for me. But at the same time, I felt deceived. I thought to myself, I am happy in here, and I don't want a big fancy future. I love it in here! Why does Mother want me to go away! But I didn't say anything out loud. In a while, Stanley and Merideth arrived and took me in their car. I kept staring at the mothers and Alex as though that might be the last time I would see them. They all waved at me as the car started moving. I wanted to wave back, but I froze. Didn't know where these strangers are taking me. Why are the mothers sending me away? I was their favorite. I was protected in the family. What about Karen? Will I ever see her again?

The Present

Four

I hadn't realized for how long I was sitting idle and dwelling in the past. The ringing of my phone pulled my mind back to the present. For an instance, I thought I was experiencing sleep drunkenness. I picked up the receiver.

"Hello, Dr. Jennifer?" the voice on the other end said as if he was trying to confirm that it's me who picked up.

"Yes, this is she," I replied.

"This is Dr. Samuel this end. If you are free, could you please come to my cabin? There is something I would like to discuss with you," said the voice on the other end.

"Yes, doctor, sure. I will be there in five," I replied respectfully.

"Thank you," he said, hanging up.

Dr. Samuel was a senior doctor at our hospital. Everyone respected him for his seniority, years of practicing experience, excellence in the job, and politeness. He is a cardiac surgeon and also the head of the cardiology department. He must be above 60 but doesn't look like it. He is a smart-looking attractive man. He has a well-proportioned and imposing appearance, suggesting good health and strength. In spite of being a very successful doctor, he has always been attached to the ground. He treated everyone with politeness, which was the most attractive quality of him that everyone would vouch for.

My interaction with Dr. Samuel was minimal. Neither our departments nor our work ever crossed paths; hence I hadn't gotten a chance to have a proper conversation with him. Though I was excited to receive a call from him, it triggered my nerves too. I couldn't speculate the reason behind that call. I walked out of my room and went directly to the nurses' station, where the night duty nurses were dozing off sitting on their seats. I knocked on their table. They jumped from their seats, scared. I smiled and said, "I'm going to meet Dr. Samuel. If there is something you can find me there, or you can always call me on my mobile. Inform Lexi too."

"Yes, doctor, will do," said one of the nurses nervously.

"Now you can go back to sleep," I said teasingly, which made the nurses giggle.

My room is on the 2nd floor, and the cardiology department is on the 3rd. As I was waiting for the elevator, I couldn't stop making my own assumptions as to why does Dr. Samuel wants to see me. When I reached the 3rd floor, I went straight to Dr. Samuel's assistant. I told her that I was called by Dr. Samuel. She pleasantly said, "Dr. Samuel is expecting you. You can go inside."

I knocked at the door, keeping my manners intact, and gently opened it. Dr. Samuel was sitting at his desk. The moment he saw me, he got up and walked towards me, extending his hand for a handshake. I humbly gave him a handshake.

He said, "Come, Dr. Jennifer, please have a seat."

"Thank you," I said.

"I was going to order a cup of coffee for me; it has been a long night. What would you like to have coffee or tea?" asked Dr. Samuel.

"Coffee is fine sir," I said.

While Dr. Samuel was on the phone, instructing his assistant to get coffees for the both of us. I took a visual tour of his cabin. He has a much bigger cabin than I. There was a glass cupboard on one corner that was filled with certificates, trophies, medals, and all his achievements. The view from his window was of a park, which gave a soothing greenery effect. But I'm sure with his position; he must be too busy with patients to sit back and enjoy the view, I thought. Apart from his desk and chair, there was a small couch and center table for visitors.

My tour was distracted by Dr. Samuel's question. At first, he asked about my department. How things were going on in there. And about some medicines that were being replaced, creating unnecessary confusion. Even though we were indulging in some vague conversations, all I was keen to know was why exactly I was here. By then, the pantry guy came in with our coffee and cookies. He placed it on the center table near the couch. As he left, Dr. Samuel gestured me to sit on the couch. We sat and comfortably drank our coffee; that's when he said, "Dr. Jennifer, I asked you to come to inform you about Mother Catherine."

I almost spit out my coffee out of shock. When Dr. Samuel asked me to see me, I presumed so many scenarios, but Mother Catherine was the last person in my mind.

"What happened to Mother Catherine? Is she here in the hospital? Is she fine?" I asked all the questions in one breath like a little girl.

"She is in the hospital right now. She was admitted today due to chest pain," replied Dr. Samuel calmly.

"We have been running some tests and conducting a few investigations and have found out that she has three blockages in the coronary artery. Two of them are complete blockages and one 80% blockage. She has to undergo bypass surgery, which will treat the blocked arteries by creating new passages for blood to flow to her heart muscle. This cannot be delayed or neglected," explained Dr. Samuel.

"You are a doctor yourself, so I don't have to explain the possibilities of the risk attached to the situation."

Dr. Samuel continued, "Mother Catherine gave your name as an emergency contact. I can get half the cost covered by medical insurance. But you will have to make the necessary arrangements for the rest. Most importantly, she needs a caring bystander during this time."

"Currently, my staff is getting her prepared for the surgery. She is in the pre-operation room. It would give her courage and relief if she meets you before the surgery," said Dr. Samuel.

"If not for Mother Catherine, I wouldn't be alive today. I was abandoned by my biological parents on the day I was born. It was Mother Catherine who saved me and gave me a home," I said with a cracked voice.

"Thank you so much, sir for arranging insurance. But the cost is not an issue. She has brought me up and made me the independent successful person I'm today. I can take care of the surgery costs. I will be by her side throughout. Please, carry on with the best treatment possible for her. I want to see her back as her old self," I said in a feeble voice. I don't know how much Dr. Samuel understood as I myself couldn't make sense of certain words I said. But he definitely understood my emotion. He gently patted my shoulder and comforted me.

He said, "Mother Catherine will be proud of you. Now let's do our duty and save her."

I quickly said a silent prayer in my mind and commenced to meet Mother Catherine. I went directly to the pre-operation room. I could see Mother Catherine from afar. She seemed too small and weak. I have never seen Mother Catherine helplessly lying down. She has always been up and on the go at all times. The bravest and most stable lady I have ever met in my life.

Apart from all the qualities as an individual, she was my mother. My mother needs me, and I will be there for her, I thought to myself. I went to her bed. The instance she saw me, she smiled. Her most loving smile.

Mother Catherine said, "Jen honey, how are you?"

"I am good, Mother, and I'm here. Don't worry about anything. Please focus on your health and getting better. I will take care of all the other stuff," I said, giving her assurance.

"I know, honey. I'm not worried. I'm ready to face what comes my way. The first time I felt pain and discomfort in my arms, back, and the neck itself, my instinct kicked, and I had a feeling this might lead to an attack. So I informed the head office, and they allocated another Mother to take up the responsibilities of the family," said Mother.

I thought to myself, she is not intimidated a tiny bit. Even during sickness, she is concerned about the inhabitants of the family. I wish I have inherited at least half her qualities in me. She is a fighter. She will overcome this phase like a champion.

We chit-chatted for a while. Mother smiled and laughed. It gave me immense pleasure to see her comfortable and at ease. At this time of pressure, we were having our own little cheerful time.

The nurses came in and requested me to leave as they had to prepare Mother for the surgery. The nurses were followed by the anesthetist.

"Mother, they are going to inject medicines in you. You will feel drowsy. You can go to deep sleep, and when you wake up, I will be here waiting for you," I said, comforting her.

She smiled and said, "OK, dear."

They injected the medicine, and Mother's eyelids were slowly shutting down. When she fell asleep, I left the room and let the doctors and nurses do their job.

I waited in front of the operation theatre. Dr. Samuel told me it might take about 4-5 hours for the surgery to be completed. I checked the time; it was 6 a.m. Albert must be awake; I will call him and inform him about Mother Catherine, I thought to myself.

Albert picked up in three rings. He was getting ready for his morning run. I told him everything in detail. He listened and said he will come by the hospital in an hour.

Meeting Mother Catherine and the stormy night jogged my childhood memories tremendously. As I waited, my thoughts went back to Stanley and Merideth.

The Past

Five

We reached Stanley and Merideth's home. It was a big house with a beautiful front yard and patio. It looked incredible. The only house I had seen till now was our child care center. But this house is incomparable to The Family. It's very well maintained and perfect. We parked our car in the garage. There was another car already parked there. "Probably, they used separate cars!" I thought. Despite everything looking perfect, I didn't have the courage to get out of the car. I wanted to go back to Mother Catherine. My mind and thoughts were stuck on the image of the mothers and Alex waving. Why did mother let me go with these strangers? Did I do something wrong? Have I been a naughty kid? Whilst I was mourning over my release from the family, Merideth held on to me and said, "Come, honey, this is your new home." That's when it hit me, and it hit me real hard. "MY NEW HOME! MY NEW HOME!" The words kept repeating themselves in my head. I got out of the car and went inside with them. There was another lady in the house. She was wearing an apron. The inside of the house was extraordinarily amazing. It was set up in a color-coordinated theme. The furniture and curtains complemented each other. They had a lavish living room with a big television.

"We have a small television in the family," I mumbled.

"You can watch your shows on the big screen now. Isn't that exciting?" asked Stanley.

"No! I like small television," I replied grumpily.

"Well…in that case, we have a surprise for you!" said Merideth in a creaking voice.

"What is it?" I asked.

"Come with me; I will show you," Merideth said, extending her arm to hold mine.

As Merideth was taking me upstairs, I saw their kitchen. It was very well equipped with a dining area attached to it. Another thing that caught my attention was the chairs. They had unusually long legs! "That's funny," I thought.

We reached upstairs. Upstairs had a long hallway and three doors. All doors were closed. I wondered what could be inside? That's when Merideth opened one of the doors. I walked in.

"WOW!" I exclaimed.

It was a magnificent bedroom with high arched windows. It had a nice, comfortable, and cozy canopy bed. There was a wardrobe in one corner, and on the opposite wall of the bed was a television. The television was smaller than the one in the living room.

"Jennifer! This is your room, sweetie. And here, you have your own television, and it's small," said Merideth lovingly.

"Mother Catherine knew these people were rich, and they could provide me a comfortable life. That's why she sent me with them. If she trusts them, I should also trust them," I thought to myself.

Merideth then took me to the other two rooms in the hallway. One was their bedroom which was bigger than mine and had a bigger bed. But I thought mine looked better. The third one was a guest room that was impressively decorated. At the end of the hallway, I saw stairs going up, but the ceiling was locked. The stairs were also narrow compared to the ones we used to come upstairs.

I asked, "Why are those stairs there when there is nothing up?"

Merideth laughed and said, "Those stairs take you to the attic. Can you see a lock hanging up in the ceiling? That's the door that opens to the attic."

"What's an attic?" I asked curiously.

"It's just an extra room up there, where we have stored some stuff that we don't need for our everyday use," replied Merideth.

"I will take you there another time. Shall we go down and eat something?" she asked.

"Yessss…" I said as I was starving.

We sat in the kitchen dining area. Stanley helped me climb the funny long-legged chair. Though it looked funny, it felt comfortable to sit. The lady in the apron had prepared some sandwiches and chocolate milk for me and coffee for Stanley and Merideth.

While passing my sandwich to me, Stanley said, "Jennifer, this is Olga; she is our house help. She cooks food and takes care of the house."

I smiled embarrassingly at Olga as this was the first time anyone had been introduced to me in a formal way.

Stanley continued, "I don't know if you are aware. Merideth and I have jobs. So we both will be out of the house during the day. We will be back by evening. So Olga will be here with you, attending to all your needs."

"Have your food," said, Stanley.

I ate the sandwiches and drank my milk. It was delicious. Honestly, the food tasted way better than the food at The Family.

As I was gulping the last drop of my milk, Olga asked, "Did you like the food, baby?"

Before I could say anything, she continued, "Please let me know whatever you like to eat or drink; I shall prepare them for you. Don't hesitate to tell me what you want."

I smiled awkwardly.

I went back to my new room, and this time, I went alone. I could feel their eyes following me. But no one came along. I guess they wanted me to get comfortable with the place.

They had bought some toys for me. I played for a while with the toys. Then I opened the curtains to see the view. It was breathtaking. From my room, I can see the front yard, which was vibrantly green and park-like. While spending time in the room, I realized that I had a bathroom attached. "This is so cool," I thought.

I decided to watch television later. As the program was running, it dawned on me that I was lonely. I used to watch this show with Karen and other children in the family. There used to be a roar of laughter at The Funny parts. I have all the comfort here, but I'm lonely. I miss Mother Catherine, Karen, and my friends. Tears rolled down my cheeks even before I could contain myself. In no time, I was sobbing out of control. I couldn't stop. That's when Merideth walked in.

I ran to Merideth, hugged her tight, and said, "please take me back. I miss them too much. I cannot live here."

Merideth consoled and comforted me. Somehow her comforting gave a sense of relief in me. She said, "let's make a phone call, and you can talk to Mother Catherine."

We called, and I spoke for a long time with Mother Catherine. She said Karen hasn't come back yet and that I should give Stanley and Merideth a chance to express their love towards me. She has always taught to keep an open mind and not face life situations with preconceived notions. She also added that I'm lucky to have been adopted by such loving people. There is one thing that Mother Catharine always says, "Opportunities don't knock at your door every day. But when it does, you have to smartly grab it."

This was my opportunity to have a comfortable life, and I grabbed it.

I felt way better after talking to Mother Catherine. Merideth had promised Mother that she would take me to the family every once a week and continue maintaining my relationships with Karen and other friends from the family. Everything seems to be working positively for me. Merideth and Stanley were willing to make any adjustments that would make me happy. Their affectionate behavior developed a ray of hope and assurance in my heart. Intuitively, I felt I might have a blissful affectionate life in my new home.

The next morning, a new day and the beginning of a new life, I was awakened by Merideth.

"Good morning, honey!" said Merideth with a radiant smile.

"Good morning Ma'am," I replied sluggishly.

Merideth paused for a moment and continued, "Did you get a good night's sleep?"

"Frankly, no. I kept tossing and turning. Don't know why. I missed having mother Catherine next to me. But it's fine, I will get better," I assured.

Merideth was surprised by the sense of maturity I had.

"OK darling, freshen up and come downstairs. We will have breakfast together." She said and left the room.

They had everything arranged for me. A new toothbrush, toothpaste, soap, towel, new dress and what not. "They are so generous." I thought.

Once I was ready I went downstairs. They were waiting for me at the patio.

"It is a pleasant morning so we thought we could sit outside and enjoy our meal." Said Stanley.

I smiled and joined them. We had cereals, fruits, toasts and orange juice. Everything tasted fresh and undoubtedly delicious. In between our meal I asked, "I thought you said you both have jobs and that you won't be home during the day. Is it a holiday today?"

"No honey, it's not a holiday. We both have taken a couple of days off so that we could be with you and make you feel at home. Once you get comfortable we will start with our routine." Replied Stanley.

"That's so thoughtful of you sir." I said respectfully.

Merideth and Stanley shared a fraction of a glance at each other.

Stanley said, "Jennifer, we have adopted you as our daughter. I know it's a lot to process for a five-year-old, but could you please not refer us as sir and ma'am! It makes us feel like strangers to you."

He continued, "We are a family now. You don't have to call us dad and mom until you feel like it, but could you call us by our names so that we would feel closer to you?"

"Yes sir…I mean…yes Stanley…" I stammered.

"That's better," said Merideth.

"Why don't we go shopping today? I can get you some new clothes. We could also get stationery for your school and probably have ice cream," said Merideth giggling.

I was excited.

"Am I going to go to school?" I asked in disbelief.

"Of course, in fact, we have already spoken to a couple of schools in town and arranged for a school tour," confirmed Stanley.

"Thank you so much, Stanley and Merideth. I can't wait to go to school," I said enthusiastically.

They were delighted when I referred them by name. They got a sense of getting one step closer to me emotionally.

We had an action-packed day. We went shopping, wandered aimlessly on the streets, ate some snacks that I didn't even know what was called, and finally, as promised, they got ice cream for me. It was a dreamy day for me. It was like serendipity. I couldn't wait to tell Mother Catherine about my day. Once we were back home, I asked them if I could call Mother. They agreed. I spoke nonstop over the phone, reminiscing every single experience of the day. Mother was amused to listen to me. Mother Catherine felt a wave of relief when she sensed the contentment in my tone. Deep in her mind, she knew she made the right choice. Stanley, Merideth, and Jennifer will make a happy family. In the end, she also mentioned that Karen will be back the next day. I said I would call the next day to talk to Karen and hung up.

Six

Karen returned back to the family after spending 10 days with her mom. She was thrilled to return, as she had so much to share with me and the mothers. The mother-daughter duo had crafted some handmade art as a gift for us. The moment she arrived, she ran to Mother Catherine, hugged her tightly, and demanded to see me.

Mother said, "Sit down, honey; I have to tell you something."

"You can tell me whatever you want Mother, but first let me please meet Jen," said Karen impatiently.

"That is exactly what I want to talk to you about," replied Mother Catherine.

Karen picked up the seriousness in Mother's tone. She instantly knew something had happened. "What is it, Mother? What happened? Is Jen alright?" asked Karen worriedly.

"Jen is fine, honey. She does not live here anymore. A loving husband and wife who couldn't conceive a baby on their own wanted to adopt Jen. Now, she lives with them." Mother Catherine said and paused for a second to study Karen's reaction.

Karen didn't flinch or say a word. So, mother went ahead and explained how everything happened and why they decided to send me along with Stanley and Merideth. Karen silently listened to every word Mother said and left the room without uttering a word.

I was gradually growing, accustomed to my new home and my room. Last night, I got better sleep than before. Gradually, my mind and body were getting acquainted with the new life. I enjoyed the meal time, as Olga made the most mouth-watering food in the world, and that was the time when we had our little conversations. This morning, during breakfast, our topic was schools. I was intrigued and had so many queries. Stanley and Merideth were happy to answer all my questions. They thought I was very inquisitive to understand the details.

Up until now, I had heard about school but had never got a chance to even pass through a school building. The thought of wearing uniforms, being with other children of my age, and studying excited me. I wanted to study. I wanted to enlighten my knowledge. I wanted to become successful. I don't know since which age I had become ambitious, but all I can remember was I'm ambitious to the core. Merideth and Stanley had said that they have planned out school tours of three different schools in town and that we will decide which one to choose after our visit. I couldn't contain my excitement. I hurriedly went up to my room to change. As I opened my wardrobe, my eyes caught attention to the small bag I had brought along with me when I came from The Family. My nostalgia was triggered. I opened the bag and saw the paper windmill I had made along with Karen. The windmill stimulated indescribable emotions in me. Abruptly, I started feeling guilty. The thought of me going to a good school while Karen continued with home schooling made me sad. I don't know for how long I sat there lost in my own world. I was jolted by a tap on my shoulder.

Merideth asked, "What happened Jenny? Why aren't you dressed yet? We have to be on time at the school."

I replied sadly, "I feel regretful to go to school. Why am I getting this fortunate opportunity and not Karen? What did I do to deserve this chance?"

Merideth sat down on the floor next to me and said, "Every person on earth has a reason and purpose for his/her life. We would learn our purpose while traveling along with the course of our living. You are chosen by God for this opportunity to serve some purpose."

She continued, "Karen will get her opportunity when the time is right for her. Even if you both grew up together in The Family, you both will have your own unique future. It's not going to be the same. Right?"

I nodded.

"Have faith in yourself. Gracefully accept the opportunity to knock at your door. And never ever feel guilty for choosing what's right for you," said Merideth.

Merideth's words made so much sense and gave me the courage to pursue my dream of going to school.

I said, "After our school visits, I will call Mother Catherine and talk to Karen too. She must have returned today."

Meanwhile, in The Family, Karen didn't speak to anyone since her return to The Family. She idly sat on her bed, staring into space, feeling lost. Mother Catherine and Mother Felicia tried their level best to make her eat or drink something. She refused and sat on her bed.

Mother Felicia asked, "Would you like to speak with Jen? We have her contact number. I can call her for you, darling."

Karen didn't reply.

You will feel good when you hear her voice…

Still no response.

They tried offering her donuts, which are her favorite, and which is something we get to eat barely once a year. They offered to take her out for a walk.

Nothing worked.

We drove to the first school. It was a huge spacious building with extremely well-planned architectural features. We parked our car and walked in through a long pathway, which was lined up with lush green well-trimmed landscape. It was a vision of a dream. As we entered the reception area, we realized there were two other families who had also come for the school tour. One family came with a boy of my age, and the other one was a girl. The boy looked nervous and was clinging to his mom. The girl seemed fine, and she smiled at me. The receptionist stepped forward and shook hands with Stanley and Merideth.

Stanley said, "Nice to meet you, I'm Stanley Walker, and I'm the one who spoke to you over the phone. Meet my wife, Merideth Walker. And this is our daughter, Jennifer Family Walker."

I was ecstatic. I was being introduced as their daughter. Stanley and Merideth gave me their surname while respecting my attachment to the family.

I have a surname...
I have a family...
I have a....mom and dad...
I'm no more the abandoned infant who survived the storm...

I was pleasantly occupied in my own delight, thankfulness, the world happiness when the receptionist held out her hand to me and said, "Hello Jennifer, nice to meet you. Welcome to "The Uptown School". I'm hoping to see you as one of our own soon."

"Thank you," I replied shyly.

Then she turned to all of us and said, "A good school is a place where children learn enough worthwhile things to make a strong start in life, where a foundation is laid that supports later learning, and where children developed the desire to learn more."

"Her introduction about school and learning sounded well-rehearsed and repeated. I'm sure she learned these lines from somewhere and uses them on everyone who visits the school," I thought.

She went on for a couple of more minutes, and then we moved to various sections of the school.

Since we were primary kids, she unveiled the primary section first. The classrooms were colorfully painted and decorated with crafts made by the students, which were interesting and impressive. The primary section had its own play area, which was not connected to the other section of the school. The hallway was long and clean with decoration hanging along the wall. The classrooms had fans, lights, benches, chairs, blackboards, and what not. Then we moved on to the other departments. It had a well-stocked library that was quiet and calm with a soothing ambiance. We also visited the well-equipped laboratories, art and craft workshops, multimedia room. When we stepped out of the building, she guided us to the sports ground for football, basketball, tennis, and volleyball. In my mind, I wondered why do Stanley and Merideth want to visit any other school? This is perfect. This has everything a kid can dream of.

After completing our visit, we returned back home. The appointment for the other two schools was the next day. The moment we reached home, I eagerly called Mother Catherine.

I asked eagerly, "Mother, has Karen come back? How is she? May I talk to her? I have a lot to tell her."

Mother replied, "Hang on, I will send someone to bring her."

Mother mumbled something to someone and came back on the phone.

"She will be here. How was your day?" she asked.

For the next few minutes, I talked non-stop about my day and the school visit as if I was participating in a monologue competition. I barely took pauses to catch my breath. Mother patiently listened to my passionate interpretation of the details. As I went on and on, she intervened and mumbled again to someone.

"Honey, Karen is in the shower. I will ask her to give you a call," said Mother lamely.

I hung up but sensed something fishy. Mother's words weren't quite convincing. Felt as though she is hiding something. Is Karen mad at me for leaving? Does she hate me? Won't she talk to me ever? All kinds of negative thoughts flashed vehemently in my head. "Or maybe she was in the shower," I thought, trying to console myself. I decided to call her later and check up on her.

Karen was still in her bed, lying under her blanket. Mother Catherine sat next to her and gently rubbed her hand over the blanket and said, "Karen honey, you cannot lay in your bed for the whole day. Please get up and eat something. I know you are sad, but you have to take care of yourself."

Karen didn't respond or even move a muscle.

Mother sighed and continued, "I know the separation from Jen is painful. You had an intense, profound connection from the very first time you saw her. I remember your first words to her; you promised to protect her like an elder sister. You both share a pure unconditional love for each other. You must be feeling lonely without her. But you should understand that God has given her an opportunity to live a comfortable life with some loving people who are wholeheartedly willing to nurture her."

"She will have a bright future. Wouldn't you be happy to see our little Jen succeeding in life?"

"When she called, I lied to her that you were in the shower. I don't think she believed me completely. Please talk to her the next time. Both of you will be happy. Now get up; I will give you something to eat or at least drink a cup of milk."

There were a few minutes of silence, and then in an inaudible feeble voice, Karen said, "I need some more time, Mother. I will come when I'm ready."

Mother thought some response is better than no response. She patted Karen's arm and left the room.

I called a couple of times only to receive made-up excuses from Mother. In the night, I asked Mother if there is an issue.

She said Karen is hurt and upset about the fact that I'm no longer living in The Family and that she hasn't spoken to anyone since. Mother assured me that everything is under control. She will talk to Karen once again the next day, and we could get in touch. It wasn't unexpected; I too would have reacted the same way if I was in her place. But I felt hopeful after my conversation with Mother. I decided to wait until the next day.

Fresh day fresh thoughts, I thought as I got up. I was occupied with my morning routine when Olga knocked at my door. She said, "Baby, come down. Someone is here to meet you."

I was over the moon.

I knew it must be Mother Catherine and Karen…

I knew she would understand…

I knew she cannot stay mad at me for long…

I thought and ran downstairs, thudding the stairs. I was stumped when I saw the lady in front of me. She wasn't Mother Catherine or Karen. Who is she?

She was a thin pale lady. She wasn't half as pretty as Meredith. Her dressing sense was mediocre.

"So, this is Jennifer!" she exclaimed sarcastically.

"You are one lucky abandoned orphan," she said.

She was about to add something to it when Merideth interfered, said firmly, "She is our daughter and nothing else."

"Yes, yes, Merideth, she is your daughter. I was just wondering how blessed she is to have you both as parents," said the lady trying to hide her jealousy.

Merideth pulled me towards her, held her arm around me, making sure I don't go anywhere near the lady, and said, "Jen honey, this is Aunty Laura. She is Stanley's sister."

We dislikingly greeted each other. Our detestation for one another, apparently for no particular reason, was clearly evident. From the look of it, I didn't think Merideth liked her either. We moved to the dining area for a breakfast. The moment I took my first bite, Laura said, "You might be eating good food after moving into Stanley's home."

"What do you eat in your orphanage for breakfast? Biscuits and black tea or previous day's leftover?" she added, mocking me.

"Laura! You are being rude. She is just a kid. I thought you came here to get to know your niece. If you continue these kinds of talks, I will have to prohibit your visits," said Merideth furiously.

Stanley walked in from his morning walk, listening to Merideth's reaction.

"What's going on?" he asked.

Merideth explained the insensitive behavior of Laura towards me. Stanley reacted protectively and said, "Laura, Jen is my daughter, and if you are not able to accept it, then please don't come here. It's fine if you are not on board with Merideth and me on this. Take your time to accept it. Because Jen is a part of us now, and we are a family. So come here only when you can be amiable and supportive."

"I'm so sorry, brother, I didn't mean any harm. Just wanted to check if Jennifer had a bad attitude. I was trying to intimidate her to perusal her reaction. She seems like a well-mannered girl," Laura responded with a fake grin.

Stanley wasn't convinced by what he heard, but he decided to ignore it and move on.

He turned to me and said, "Jen honey, today we have to visit the other two schools. Get ready once you finish your breakfast."

I gobbled the food and ran upstairs. I didn't want to spend a single minute in the same room as Laura.

Laura had decided to tag along with us in the car as she had some shopping plans. She lived in the outskirts and took a bus to commute. I didn't like the idea but didn't really have a choice. How much ever time Laura spent in our house, she made sure for me to realize how undeserving I was of everything I received. She would stare every time I touched anything in the house. She goggled enviously at my dress. It was a pretty dress Merideth had got me. With every look and movement, she made sure I comprehended that I wasn't welcome in her life.

On our way, we dropped Laura off and visited the other two schools. All the schools were equally good with well-equipped modern amenities. After coming back home, all three of us sat on the patio to discuss our school visits and to decide which one to choose. After putting forward our thoughts, we finally decided to go with The Uptown school, which had all the amenities and was closer to home than the other two.

Mother Catherine was sitting in her office doing some work. It was a busy day for her as the head office was planning on making some changes in the regular paperwork method. Karen knocked and walked in. Mother was pleased to see her.

"Come, darling, take a seat," Mother said lovingly.

Karen said gloomily, "I miss Jen. I miss being around her. I miss playtime with her. I miss her a lot. But I know she has been blessed with this enormous life-changing opportunity that would enlighten her future. So I'm happy for her. I love her, and I want her to have a glorious life."

"I'm sad and lonely, but I will be fine. Like you always say, time heals the pain," she added, smiling.

"Next time when Jen calls, I would love to talk to her," she said.

"I'm so proud of you my darling. I knew all my children have a golden heart. You all are my treasure," said Mother Catherine taking pride in her children.

Seven

I called up Karen, and we spoke for a long time. In the beginning, it was basically crying and sobbing, which gradually led to chit-chatting, and soon I was telling her everything about the school and my new life. She told me she had a good time with her mom. Her mom has been showing some improvement health-wise too. Karen promised me that she would come and visit me and my home. I told her I would love to go to The Family and spend some time with her. We decided we would make some plans with the permission of the adults.

"The school will soon be opening. Let's better hurry and buy you new uniforms and stationary," said Stanley excitedly.

"Yeah! Let's do that," joined Merideth.

At first, we went to the school store and bought uniforms and books. Later, we shopped in a nearby shopping mall for stationery, lunch box, water bottle etc.…

It was an exciting day. We had so much fun shopping for me. Sometimes, I wonder is this all happening for real or am I in a dreamland. Then I see the way Merideth and Stanley look at me. Every time their eyes lay on me, it overflows with love, care, and affection. They are my guardian angels. "I will always make them proud of me," I promised myself.

Within a couple of days, the school opened, and I started going to school. I admired every aspect of the school experience and took esteem pride to be able to attend school. No one in my class or school knew about my past or about my adoption. As per the school policy, they had kept all those pieces of information discreet. Everyone thought I was Stanley and Merideth's daughter, and so no one treated me differently, which made it easier for me to mingle and make new friends. In a twinkling of an eye, I became everyone's favorite. Almost my whole class was my friend, and the teachers liked me too for my respectful behavior and studious nature. I was well focused on my studies and always completed all my tasks on time. Whenever I receive an appreciation, or when I perform well in school, the first thought that occurs to me is I hope Stanley and Merideth would be proud. Subconsciously, I did everything to either impress them or make them happy. There have been days when I wondered if my biological parents would have loved me as much as Merideth and Stanley!

One day, along with my classmates, I was playing in our play area. We were having a fun time when I slipped from a slide and fell hard on the ground. I hit my arm so hard on the ground that I broke my wrist bone. It was tremendously painful. I couldn't stop crying. The school nurse examined me and said it seems like a fracture and that I should be taken to the hospital for a cast. The school informed Stanley and Merideth, and they agreed to come directly to the hospital. The hospital was a scary place. Everyone around seemed to be walking with a serious face. They were all strangers. Except for the school nurse, I didn't know anyone, which made me feel insecure and fearful. As we were waiting outside the doctor's office, I could see from afar Merideth and Stanley approaching with a worried faces. Seeing them felt like absorbing a painkiller. I was relieved and not scared anymore, as I knew the two people who would protect me from any danger are there.

The doctor examined me and took an X-ray. I had fractured my wrist. The doctor said that I will need to be put on a cast, as it will hold my broken bone in place and prevent the area from movements. Luckily, it was my left arm, and I'm a right-handed person, so I was able to program as normal. The doctor added that I should rest at home for three days and then get back to my normal school routine. I had to wear the cast for four weeks.

We returned home. I went upstairs to my room and rested. The next couple of weeks, my life and my perspective towards life, family, relations took a substantially pivotal change. I was poured with care, profound love, selfless unconditional love, and attention. Merideth and Stanley took off from work and stayed at home to take care of me. Even though I was fine and was able to function normally with my other arm, Merideth insisted on feeding me at times which I gladly agreed to, as I enjoyed the attention I was receiving. Those couple of weeks evoked a deep sensation of love and family in me. It was during one of those times when Merideth was feeding me that I called her MOM. I immediately realized that I wasn't just verbally calling her that I called her mom from my heart with intense deep emotions. Merideth conceived my intensity when I said, mom. Merideth couldn't withhold her tears. She hugged me and sobbed like 'a child who had unexpectedly recovered his lost favorite toy.' I realized how much that meant to her. She had been waiting her whole life to hear that. Stanley was quietly listening to our conversation, sitting on the couch in the corner of the room. His eyes were facing down. I knew he was overwhelmed. I went up to him, sat on his lap, resting my head on his chest, and said, "I am so blessed to have you both as my parents. I will always be grateful to you for choosing me. Thank you, Dad." It was an emotionally happy day for us. Like it's said, "All is well that ends well," but the only fact was that this wasn't the end.

Months and years passed. I was living an unbelievably dreamy life. Mom and dad were the most amazing people on earth. They valued my relationship with the inhabitants of The Family and so openly encouraged me to visit them and spend time with them during holidays. At times, Karen came home for sleepovers. Those were the most amazing nights. We talk for most of the night and then watch a horror movie together and end up spending a sleepless night scared to death. Life was good except for Aunty Laura's exasperating visits. She hasn't accepted me as a family member, and she still looks at me as someone who accidentally got lucky at her brother's expense. She pinpoints fault in anything and everything I do. Gradually, I learned the way to cautiously handle her and not let her words or actions affect my ecstatic life. She excels in executing sugar-coated poisoned words. At first, it sounds like a compliment, but it has a hidden taunt in it. She, without fail constantly, makes it a point to make me feel worthless during her every visit.

It was my sixteenth birthday. Mom & Dad have planned an eventful day. They have been planning and scheming behind my back to surprise me. They are too cute to conceal their excitement. They have been acting kiddish and jumpy every time I walked in. But I let them believe that I wasn't aware of their plans.

All these years were the best years of my life. Like Mom always said, I was growing into a fine-looking girl. I had an above-average height, well-defined cheekbones, and strong jawlines. My breasts were finely shaped with a thin waist. I was pretty attractive, I must say. Sometimes, Mom says my biological parents must have been good-looking, as I have inherited a few good looks. Dad adored my curious eyes. Every time I had a query, even before I asked him, he would know it, and when I ask him how he knows, he would teasingly say, I can read it in your curious eyes. My dad was my best friend. I could share anything with him except for one thing. I had a huge crush on this boy in my class. I was too shy to talk about it to anyone. I haven't even shared it with my friends. I get so nervous around him and act stupid. So to avoid any kind of senseless stupid conversation, I ignore him completely. The only person I have shared this with is Karen. She is my soul sister, and intuitively, she finds out my thoughts.

The best quality in me was my interest in education. From primary school, I was good at my studies. With age, I only got better at it. I had this quest to become successful in life. It could be an impact of me being abandoned instantly after birth. I had a strong yearning to grow up into an independent accomplished lady who can take care of herself and wouldn't need to depend on anyone. I grew up to be tremendously ambitious, and by now, I knew what I wanted to become. I wanted to become a doctor, not just a doctor. A doctor that would help ladies give birth. Even before I knew the word Gynecologist, I was unquestionably absolute that I wanted to become one. I studied and worked hard with that aim. Mom and Dad know about my dream, and they have promised to support and guide me throughout the way.

My birthday was in two days. It was challenging to act normal around mom and dad, knowing they were planning a surprise party for me. Mom bought me a beautiful floral dress and a photo album scrapbook. She asked me to fill the album with my most cherished moments. It was such a thoughtful gift, I thought. Dad gave me a laptop, saying as I have so much research work to do, I could use my own laptop. He said, "I'm going for a business trip on your birthday, that's why I'm giving you your gift in advance." I was on top of the world and couldn't stop myself anymore.

I giggled and said, "Come on, Mom Dad, I know you guys are planning a party. You both are too cute to hide anything from me."

"You knew about that!" squeaked Mom.

"OK, hence the kitten is out of the box, we might as well plan the event together," said Dad.

"Were you serious about your trip, Dad?" I asked.

"Yes, honey, I will be traveling the next day of your birthday," replied dad.

I invited some of my friends from school, Karen, Mother Catherine and Mother Felicia, from my side. Mom and Dad invited a few of their colleagues and friends. We didn't want a party planner to decorate the house as we thought it to be a family bonding time. Preparing for an event is a happy time, which we wanted to spend together. We decorated the house with balloons, flowers and some fancy lights. Mom ordered the cake, and Olga had a whole menu planned for the day.

Mother Catherine and Felicia, and Karen were the first to arrive. Karen said I looked beautiful in my new dress. She teased me, saying I'd dressed up to impress my crush. I told her I haven't invited him. She was disappointed, as she hadn't met him yet. She was hoping to meet him. As the rest of the guests arrived, the party got exciting and happening. We had karaoke and had set up a dance floor. I'm sure our neighbors might have used earplugs that night as some of us sang terribly. But we were having fun, so no one cared about the rhythm. As always, Olga was the star of the night as she was at her best in preparing her delicacies. Overall, it was a heavenly night that was happening for real. After all the guests left, I told Mom and Dad that I wanted to add some pictures in my scrapbook and went to my room. I had clicked some pictures using Dad's instant photo camera. I added the beautiful moments I had captured during the party. It was the most momentous day of my life.

Eight

The next day, Dad got ready to leave for his trip. He was planning to go for four days. It's a part of his job. He often travels. So packing and getting ready was a regular routine for him. We had breakfast together, and he left. He promised he would call once he lands. After he left, I went to school, and mom got back to the office. It was a regular uneventful day. Olga was busy cleaning the house after the previous day's havoc.

When I came back from school, Olga told me that Mom came early from work. I asked her if everything was OK. She said, "Madam has a headache, maybe it's because of the late-night party yesterday."

"She is sleeping in her room," added Olga.

"Let me go and check. I promise I won't make noise if she is sleeping," I said.

As I was about to step up, I heard Mom coming down.

She saw me and said, "Hi honey, how was your day."

Before I could say anything, Mom's phone rang, which she was carrying in hand.

She answered, "Hello!…What!…What are you saying? Are you…are you sure…?"

The phone slipped from mom's hand, clattering down the stairs. Her vision blurred with tears, and a wave of overwhelming grief and shock engulfed her. She took a step backward, her foot missing the edge of the step. Her body swayed, unbalanced, as she reached out desperately for the railing but missed. With a gasp, she tumbled down the stairs, her body twisting painfully with each impact. The world around her seemed to slow down, a surreal blend of physical pain and emotional agony. She landed at the bottom with a sickening thud, hear head striking the marble floor. Darkness crept into the edges of her vision as she lay there, her mind still reeling from the devastating news. Soon she drifted to an unconscious state, her body crumpled at the foot of the stairs, her face pale and tear streaked.

"MOM!" I screamed.

"MA'AM!" Olga Screamed.

We both tried our best to wake her, but she remained unconscious. I could hear someone on the other end of her phone. I ran to the phone and picked it up.

I said, "Hello, this is Jennifer. I'm Merideth's daughter. Who is this? What did you say? Mom fell down the stairs, and she is unconscious now."

"Hello Jennifer, I called to deliver some sad news. Mr. Stanley Walker's plane crashed while landing. Mr. Stanley was immediately given emergency medical care, but unfortunately, he didn't make it," said the man. In just a few moments, my life shattered. Everything fell apart. Images of Dad and us having breakfast in the morning and him leaving the house flashed in front of my eyes. I stood there devastated and shocked without moving a muscle. In the background of my thoughts, I could hear Olga, talking calling the ambulance.

I didn't have much time to mourn for Dad; Mom needed me. Olga and I tried to wake Mom but failed.

Olga asked, "Who was on the phone? What's going on?"

I simply stared at her, struggling to get words out of my mouth. Olga sensed something terrible has happened. Even before I said anything, tears flowed down her cheeks.

"What is it, baby? You are scaring me! Please say something!" She asked, terrified.

"Dad's plane crashed. He…hhhee didn't make it," I said, wailing.

Olga said nothing. She was in dismay.

The ambulance arrived, and we went to the hospital. Mom got admitted. She was still unconscious. After running some basic tests, the doctor said he wanted to talk to me.

He asked, " Where is your Dad? Will he be coming now?"

I looked down, sobbing, and said, "No, he won't come."

The doctor understood what I meant. He didn't ask anything else about Dad. He inquired if there was any other elder person in the family he could talk to. I told him it was just me.

He said worriedly, "I see. How did your mother get the injury?"

I told in detail that had happened.

He said, "Jennifer, it's a serious situation. I have no choice but to pass on the information to you due to the absence of any other adult. We have to do an MRI scan to get a detailed report of your mother's injury. It doesn't look good. If you have any relatives or friends, please call them. It's going to take a while."

I informed Mother Catherine. She came to the hospital with Karen. Seeing them, my repressed shock and sadness surfaced. I lay on Mother's lap and bawled out unrestrainedly. Mother and Karen tried their level best to console me, but nothing worked. I was unstoppable until the doctor came.

The doctor had a worried look on his face. He looked at Mother and asked if she was with Merideth. She said yes.

He said, "The fall has caused severe damage to Ms. Walker's brain. She has a cerebral hemorrhage which is uncontrolled bleeding in the brain. This has occurred from the injury she got when she hit her head on the railing. She is still unconscious. She has to undergo emergency surgery to drain out the blood clots and relieve pressure. Or else it could be life-threatening."

He paused, giving us time to take in the information he was passing, and then continued.

"The surgery does not guarantee 100 percent recovery. We could expect different results depending on various other medical conditions of the patient," he said.

"What do you mean different results?" I asked curiously.

He said, "Some patients experience difficulty with memory, reading writing, or comprehension.

"Some have permanent loss or changes in vision. Partial paralysis or unconsciousness and coma are other results.

"I'm not saying Ms. Walker will definitely experience these complications, but I'm just warning you that it could happen. Avoiding the surgery completely is life-threatening. Some patients recover with the least complications. It's my duty to explain every aspect of it," explained the doctor.

"She has also fractured her leg, for which we have to put a cast for 3-4 weeks," he said.

"We are preparing her for the surgery," said the doctor and left.

"Mother! Yesterday, I had a happy family. It was the most beautiful day of my life, and today everything has fallen apart. Dad has gone…Mom is in this situation! Why is this happening?" I reacted.

"Have faith, my baby, stay strong. Your mom needs you the most today. You are her strength and probably the only reason to survive. In her situation, willpower is extremely important to fight, and you are the only one who can give her that," Mother advised.

The surgery took around 10 hours to complete. As I waited in the long hospital lobby my mind began to drift, seeking solace in the precious memories we shared. I remembered how my dad taught me to ride a bike in the park close to our home that was once filled with love and laughter. I could still hear his encouraging words and the laughter we shared when I finally balanced on my own. I proudly rode my bike towards him where he would be standing with his arms outstretched to catch me if I fell. The memory of his proud smile filled my hearth with a bittersweet warmth. I recalled the time we had gone camping under the stars, mom pointed out constellations and telling stories about each one while dad made funny comments annoying mom. They were so cute when they argued over silliest matters. I used to imagine meeting a life partner like mom and dad who completed each other. Tears streamed down my face as I clung hard to these memories, and suddenly it struck me those have become memories and those beautiful moments are going to stay there forever in my memory. Suddenly I felt the depth of my love for mom and dad and without realizing I said out loud "I love you mom and dad. Please don't leave me and make me an orphan again."

Immersed in my own world I felt the soft touch on my shoulder. It was the doctor. The doctor said Mom is stable and that they could remove the clots. Now, we wait for her to wake up to know if the surgery has had any impact on her. As per Mother Catherine's advice, I had called Aunty Laura to tell her about Dad and Mom. The moment she arrived, she hugged me and said she is here to take care of things and that I didn't have to worry about anything. It was shocking to see her being supportive. But then, I figured she had always loved Dad. So it could be possible that her concerns are genuine. We were all exhausted. Aunty Laura sent Olga back home to prepare food for us. She asked Mother and Karen if they would like to leave too, but they refused and stayed with me. We waited for a couple of hours more. The doctor called us to his room. I introduced Aunty Laura to the doctor. He seemed surprisingly relieved to talk to an adult who is related to the patient, which indicated that he is going to deliver difficult news.

He said, " The surgery was a success, and since we were able to remove the clot, Ms. Walker's life is out of danger."

He turned to me and said, "But as I had explained earlier about certain consequences."

"Ms. Walker also has had an impact. She has slipped into a coma. We still have hope. She could come out of the coma in a day, a couple of weeks, or even a year. It's unpredictable but attainable. Just continue with her medications and stay positive."

I was devastated. It felt like life has taken a complete U-turn from what it was the previous day. Did I just lose both my parents? All of a sudden, I'm alone again. As I was walking the hospital hallway lost in thoughts, I happened to read a message on one of the wall decors. It said, "Change is Inevitable." Yes, my life has changed. My mom's life has changed. And I'm not going to be scared of change. When I had nothing, Mom and Dad gave me their hand to hold, shoulder to rely on, and lots of love to be happy. I wouldn't have had any of these comforts if it weren't for Mom and Dad. My mom is helpless, and she needs my hand to hold on to. And I will do everything to bring her back to normal life. I pledged to myself.

In a couple of days, Mom got discharged, and we came home. Olga and I had prepared her room well, keeping in mind her requirements. The ambulance staff helped in placing mom on her bed. Her eyes were closed all the time as if she was sleeping. But the doctor said she could sense and hear us. I had decided that I would talk to her every day and tell her about my school and friends to keep her brain alive. Before we brought Mom home, Aunty Laura took care of Dad's funeral. I must say she did a decent job. It was hard for me, but out of the blue, I felt stronger and more courageous to face it. Aunty Laura is still staying with us. Though I kept wondering why she wouldn't leave as she has a husband and a son back home. Wouldn't she want to see them? I thought. Anyways, let her do whatever she wants; I will give all my attention to mom, I decided.

During the day, Olga took care of mom, and once I was back from school, I took the responsibility of giving her medicines on time, changing her pads, cleaning her up, etc. My day and night started passing by really fast as I was occupied by school, studies, and Mom. Aunty Laura was still at home. She would try to have conversations with me at times, which I don't entertain much. One day, while I was busy doing my homework, she walked in and said, "I'm thinking of bringing my husband and my son Jack here. For how long will we live apart! They can come here, and we can all live together."

I was shocked by her decision. Here, I'm having a hard time having Aunty Laura around; how will I be able to tolerate her husband and son, whom I have met barely twice.

I said as politely as I could, "I can manage the situation here by myself. I'm so grateful that you have been here during our tough times. The way you managed everything was extremely helpful. But I think I can take it from here."

"And as you said, it's unfair to leave uncle Paul and Jack by themselves for so long. If you wish, you could go back home. I can take care of Mom and home," I added.

I could see that my reply didn't make her happy. She stared at me for a moment, and it was like I could literally hear her saying, "how dare you to talk to me like you are the owner of the house?"

After a pause, she said affirmatively, "Uncle Paul and Jack are coming to stay here, and we are going to live here, and that's final."

I defenselessly sat mute. I could apprehend that she is plotting something. I had no idea about my parents' finances, and since I'm a minor, I don't have any right to their earnings or property. Since she is planning to bring her family and settle in our home, I'm sure she is scheming something about the money and property too. I didn't know what to do. I couldn't get any guidance from Mom too. Then I thought maybe since I don't like her, I'm being skeptical. Maybe her intentions are genuine. Anyway, I have a lot on my plate now. Will see how things head.

Within two days, uncle Paul and Jack came home. Uncle Paul was a big man. He was tall and unhealthily big. His head was bald, and he had evil eyes. Every time he spoke to me, his eyes went to all the wrong places that made me uncomfortable. Jack seemed like a nice boy. He was one year older than me. He was an introvert which was the exact opposite of his parents. He spoke only when spoken to and was good in studies that's what I've heard about him. When they saw me, Jack said, "I'm sorry, Jenny, for what happened. Stay strong. Your mom needs you."

I said, "Thank you, Jack."

Uncle Paul came closer and put his arms around me and said, "I'm sorry dear, don't worry about anything. We are here to support you during this hard time. We will get through this together." As he said these words, his hand kept rubbing all over my back. It went up and down a couple of times. I tried to free myself from his grip, but it was like a vulture gripping on its prey. But the moment his hand went further down to my buttocks, I pushed him as hard as I could and freed myself. I didn't reply anything to him and ran quickly to my room.

I locked the door behind me, still trying to catch my breath. I felt dirty and annoyed. I realized that I'm not safe in my own home anymore. I should be vigilant. I have no other choice than strongly resist any kind of unwelcome behavior. As long as my mom is lying motionless, there I've to tolerate these vultures. I sneaked into Mom's room and fed her night medicine along with her liquid food that's attached to the nasal tube. I quietly returned to my room, locked the door, and went off to sleep. I didn't want to go down for dinner. No one cared if I ate or not. I thought if it was Mom or Dad, they would have forced me to eat and would never let me go to bed starving. I have no idea for how long I kept weeping. Finally, I fell asleep tired and exhausted.

Nine

The next morning, I got ready for school and went downstairs. I walked up to the kitchen dining area and sat there. But Olga didn't come with breakfast. I called out her name but with no response. Aunty Laura walked in from outside and said, " Ah, you got ready for school! Today, we are coming along with you to your school. I want to get Jack admitted in there."

"Where is Olga?" I asked.

"I let her go. We don't need her anymore. Why should we pay a salary to someone when there is so little work in this house, which you and I can manage easily? We should keep in mind that Stanley is not around, and Merideth is in no position to work," she replied nonchalantly.

"But Olga was not just a servant. She was like a family member," I said, unbelievably surprised about what Aunty Laura had done.

"You mean just like you," she said with a wicked look.

I knew my future days are going to be terribly painful. But I made up my mind. Whatever they are planning to do or however; they will torture me, I won't leave. My mom needs my support. I don't trust these people, and I won't leave my mom. They can try all kinds of dirty tricks on me to kick me out of the house, but I will not go.

They tagged along with me to school. Deep in my mind, I prayed and hoped that Jack wouldn't get admission to the school. At least that could be a reason for them to go back to their town. But I went to my class and couldn't know what happened in the school office until evening. In the evening, when I reached home, the house was a mess. The kitchen sink was filled with dirty dishes, and the counter was unclean with leftover food all around.

"Thank God you are back," said Aunty Laura.

"I don't know why I have a severe headache. Can you please clean the house?" she asked dramatically.

I'm not a fool; I knew what was happening and what she was trying to do. But I didn't express anything. "I will never let her know what I'm thinking," I thought to myself.

"Sure, not a problem," I said, and I cleaned the whole house.

It took almost two hours for me to complete my work. I then quickly went to Mom, cleaned her, and gave her medicines. She had passed a lot of urine and even stool, which made the whole room stinky. The condition in which I found Mom, I doubted if Aunty Laura even gave her anything to eat or even came upstairs. Mom cannot physically eat food, but we have to feed her the liquid food via a nasal tube. That made me wonder what will happen to Mom when I'm at school. I don't trust Aunty Laura or uncle Paul to feed her or give her medicines on time. While I was lost in my thoughts, I heard Aunty Laura call out my name. "I will just be back," I told Mom.

Aunty Laura said, " Do you know how to cook? I'm sure you know how to make sandwiches. Just make some sandwiches for everyone."

I said, "Sure!"

I prepare dinner for everyone. Had my sandwich and cleaned the kitchen. By the time I finished all the work, I was exhausted. I tried to do my homework, but I could barely focus and fell asleep on my book.

The next morning, I realized I had incomplete homework. "This was the first time ever I would be going to school without completing my work," I thought. I quickly got ready. When I went downstairs, no one was there. They must have gone for their morning walk. I quickly prepared serials and cut an apple, and had my breakfast. Then went upstairs, changed Mom's urine bag, wiped her clean, and left before they returned. But while in school, all I could think of was Mom. "Will Aunt Laura give her anything to eat? Will she clean her up in case she passes the stool? Will she give her medications on time?" I couldn't focus on my class or teacher throughout the day. My teachers were surprised to note that I hadn't completed my homework. I'm the topper of my class and even my school. Teachers refer me as an example to other students as an inspiration. My teachers were aware of Dad's untimely demise and Mom's health fiasco. They knew my life was in a debacle at the moment. So they let this one pass.

When I reached back home, Aunty Laura seemed unhappy. She gave an annoyed look and said, "Why did you leave without preparing breakfast?"

I replied shockingly, "I have to be at school on time, and I assumed you would make it!"

She sat down on the couch with her legs crossed and commanded with a firm loud voice, "So, here is how it's going to happen. From today onwards, you have to do everything Olga used to do in this house. You will cook, clean, and do the laundry. Set up an alarm plan for your day as per your wish. And if you dare to complain about any of this or even utter a word about things happening in this house to anyone, I will stop your mother's medications. I'm the closest relative, and I have the authority to run this house and make financial and medical decisions as per law. You better follow my command and act wisely for your mother's sake. You are a smart girl but don't try to be clever with me."

"But...but..."

"But what, Jennifer? Do you want your mother to get better or stay in bed forever?" she shouted.

I looked down and muttered, "I want her to get better."

"Then just do what I say," she replied and smiled victoriously.

I was smoldering with resentment. Her smile was maddening. If I could, I would snatch her tongue out so that she could never talk in her life. I ran upstairs to my room and slammed the door behind me. Rage was flowing through like lava in me. But I couldn't react. I was helpless. Mom's life was on the line. Before I could think or plan, she called out to me to clean up the house and prepare dinner. I did as she said without resentment.

After finishing all the work Aunty Laura asked me to do, I came back to my room. I stayed up all night planning my course of action under the current circumstance. In my mind, I analyzed the situation. I came to the conclusion that I have to bear with these vicious people for a while for the safety of Mom. As she said, she does have the legal right since she is the closest relative, and she has an upper hand over us currently. If I try to resist or upset Aunty Laura or Uncle Paul, they could take all Dad and Mom's money and disappear.

Instead, if I patiently handle them for two years until I turn 18, I would be able to save at least some of my parents' earnings for my mom when she recovers. Or miraculously, if mom recovers quickly, then everything will be solved. I should be smart and not impulsive. Having patience at the moment can benefit me and Mom in the long run, or else we could lose everything to these vultures. I decided to go with the flow and nod to all the things Aunty Laura would ask me to do. Let her keep guessing what my plans are.

The next morning, I was the first one to wake up in the house. I did the morning chores and prepared breakfast for everyone. As I was just about to leave for school, Jack came out of their room, wearing my school uniform. "Oh! So he got admission!" I thought disappointingly.

"I guess we will be going to school together," Jack said, smiling.

I liked Jack. He was nothing like his parents. He was polite with words and minds his own business.

"I guess so," I said, and we got into the car.

Uncle Paul was driving the car. Jack sat in the front seat with him. I sat at the back. Uncle Paul positioned the rearview mirror in such a way that he could get a clear reflection of me. I was uncomfortable throughout the ride to school, as he wouldn't stop looking at me and smiling sneakily. Jack didn't pay attention to what was happening as he was going through the school diary and trying to learn the rules and regulations to be followed.

Nearly a month passed. My energy got drained out with all the household work and studies and running around to the store for grocery shopping. I had a schedule to complete all the work on time and yet every day, my school work remained incomplete. I was descending in my education standard. Whenever I sat down to study, Aunty Laura would purposely send me to the store to get something or give me extra work to do. I was juggling and struggling with the housework and school work. Apart from all that, my greatest fear was Mom's deteriorating health. While I was at school, she wasn't being cleaned or given medicine on time. And I even doubt if she was being fed the whole day. She suffered from bedsores and infections. She needed to be treated for that. When I asked Aunty Laura about Mom, she said, "She is your mother. You figure out a solution for this. I'm not going to let you keep a servant for her."

As per legality, I had two more years of tolerance with these people. I seriously gave the thought of taking a break from school for a year and being with Mom prioritizing her health. Once I turn 18, I can apply for custody of the property and take decisions on my own. I met with the school principal and talked to him about my idea of taking a year break from school. He was impressed and proud of me. He said, "In today's time, people are so self-absorbed, and here, you are a brilliant student, wholeheartedly intending to leave school to take care of the parent. I'm delighted to have a student like you in my school."

He then added, "I think there is another option for you. You can continue with home learning and finally come to school to give your exams. You won't be provided with any study materials, as you are not paying the fee. You will have to arrange your own study materials. But if you can pay the exam fee, you will be allowed to come to the school and give exams. And if you pass, you will be eligible to go to the next class. In that way, you won't miss out on time."

"But I will have to discuss with the board regarding the same. Would you be interested in doing so?" asked the principal.

"I think I could do that," I replied, happy and relieved.

"OK then, I will confirm with you once I get approval from the board," assured the principal.

I didn't talk to anyone about my plan. Usually, I tell Mom everything but somehow didn't say anything about this. Because I thought she might feel guilty as I was making this decision for her.

On the next working day, the Principal called me up to his office and told me I could do home learning and apply just for the exams alone by the end of the year. I was happy. I didn't regret it a tiny bit as I knew I was doing the right thing. I told my closest friends in the class about my mom's deteriorating health and my decision to leave the school at least for a year. They sincerely agreed to help me with my studies and promised to share study materials with me. They said, "We will take turns and drop the textbooks at your place during the weekends. We will also inform you about the links and websites for reference." I thanked them for being supportive.

While leaving for home, I met Karen at the school gate. I was surprised to see her. In all the melodrama in my house, I had completely forgotten to call her or talk to her.

I asked, "What are you doing here?"

She replied, "I came to your house twice last week, and I called up so many times. Every time that Laura picked up and said you were busy. You never returned my calls too. I got worried. Are you OK, Jen?"

"OH KAREN!" I sighed and hugged her so tight and burst out into tears. I was holding on to my emotions for so long that it overflowed like a waterfall on a rainy day. Karen sensed my pain, and instead of bombarding me with questions, she just hugged me back and let me cry it out. Honestly, it felt good.

We sat down under the tree on my campus, and I told her everything that had been happening, including my decision to leave school.

"Why are you leaving school for that barbarous lady. Who does she think she is? I will come there and whack that demented head of hers and punch her nose until she bleeds!" squealed Karen.

"Honey, why don't you come to the family and live there. Bring your mom. We are all there. We will take good care of her with the limited facilities we have. At least she will be safe. I will talk to Mother Catherine. I'm sure she will agree," said Karen, concerned.

"No, hon, if she knows I shared this information with anyone, she would harm Mom. I don't have any proof against her. For the outside world, she has left her home, and her whole family is living with us to support us during this tough time. In addition to that, she is the one handling Dad and Mom's finances and properties. If we leave, she and the dirty husband of hers would take all the hard-earned money of my parents. It's my responsibility to protect what's theirs for my mom," I explained.

"I'm so proud of you, Jen. And don't worry, I'm here. Whatever you need, just name it. You know I will always be there for you right?" Karen asked lovingly.

"Yes. You are my rock," I said.

I didn't bother to inform Aunty Laura about my decision. She inquired the next day why I wasn't going to school. I told her that I quit. I could see the delight in her eyes. I said I wanted to be with my mom rather than in school. Jack felt bad about my decision. He came to my room that night and said, "Jenny, I know my parents are being hard on you. And it's because you don't trust them around your Mom that you have decided to do home learning. I'm sorry you are having to take such a decision. Please, let me know if I could help you in any way. I can borrow books from the school library or arrange some study materials or whatever you need. But please, don't tell my parents I'm helping you. They won't like it."

"That's so thoughtful of you, Jack. Thank you. I will let you know if I need anything," I responded.

Weeks proceeded, and I got used to my new routine of doing the household chores and home learning. My friends, as promised, helped me with study materials. I was in year 11, and my syllabus was relatively tough. So it was getting harder to learn on my own. But I wasn't going to give up. Jack also sneakily helped me at times with my work. He was one year senior to me and was good in his studies.

One day, unexpectedly, I saw my crush standing at the front door of my house. I was in my room upstairs and saw him from my room window. He had rung the doorbell and waited for someone to answer the door. I was surprised to see him. I had a huge crush on him but never even spoke to him.

"What is he doing here? Oh my God, what do I do?" I wondered and started panicking.

I didn't want Aunty Laura to open the door and be rude to him. So I quickly went downstairs. Before leaving the room, I checked myself in the mirror. "I look hideous," I thought. But I don't have time to change or freshen up. I opened the door, stepped outside, and shut the door behind me before Aunty Laura arrived.

I said, "Hi Albert, how are ya?"

I tried really hard to sound cool and stylish, but it didn't sound cool at all.

He smiled and said, "I'm good. How about you?"

Somehow, I felt that he was even more nervous than me. Why is he nervous! I wondered.

He continued, "I came to know from our classmates that you have decided to do home learning. I'm here to let you know I want to help."

"Oh, that's so sweet. Thanks. I have the books for now. Will let you know if I need anything else," I replied.

"I want to give you my number. You can call me whenever you want," he said shyly.

He had come with his number written down on a piece of paper. I couldn't believe what just happened. In all the tension that was going on, Albert's presence changed the whole atmosphere. Suddenly, the door opened, and Aunty Laura came out.

"Who are you? And what do you want?" she asked rudely.

"I'm Jennifer's classmate, and I came to share some notes with her," replied Albert politely.

"She doesn't need anyone's notes. You can leave," she said.

Albert stared at me in dismay and began to leave.

"No…wait…" I stammered.

"It's OK. Take care," he said and left.

"Why did you behave like that? He was here to offer help!" I told Aunty Laura.

"I will talk however I want. You don't teach me. Now go inside and do the laundry," she said arrogantly.

Albert changed my mood completely. I was on cloud nine for the rest of the day. I didn't mind doing my boring chores. At night, before going to bed, I went to Mom and had a chat with her. I talked to her about random stuff. We were reminiscing our days with Dad. I took out the photo album scrapbook and went through the most memorable day of my life, my 16th birthday, and remembered how happy we were.

The Present

Ten

I shut down my scrapbook, reminiscing the time with Dad. My tears flowed down without my permission. I felt a tiny soft hand on my face wiping out my tears.

"Don't cry, Mommy; the storm is gone. Look outside, it's sunny. Don't be scared. You are a brave girl!" said Ria innocently.

Children are pure souls. They are a precious gift from God. Ria was talking about the actual storm outside, but I felt she was being diaphanous.

I smiled, put her on my lap, and said, "You are right, sweetie. The storm has passed. I'm not scared anymore. I have you with me, my brave little angel."

She timidly said, "I will protect you, Mommy."

"Whom did we meet at the hospital today? Why did she have some tubes on her? Is she going to be OK?" asked Ria.

"She is Mother Catherine. She is like a mother figure to me. I love and respect her a lot. She was unwell, for which she needed to undergo surgery. She is doing fine now. Those tubes are to support her with feeding food and intake of medicines which she cannot do by herself right now. Once she feels even better, it will be removed," I told.

"But I thought granny is your mother!" exclaimed Ria, confused.

"Yes, sweetie, Granny is my mother. But Mother Catherine also gave me the love and protection of a mother, so I look at her as a mother figure. I will explain it in detail once you grow up a little more. I'm sure you will like my story," I explained.

While we were having a mother-daughter time, we heard the door being opened. Albert sneaked into the house. He was surprised to see us.

"You didn't go to bed, Jen! You were up all night babe, get some rest!" said Albert.

"I couldn't sleep. The whole night has jogged a lot of memories," I said.

Albert playfully sent Ria to her room. He sat next to me and put his arm around me. I rested my head in his chest like a baby. That is the most secure place on earth for me. Albert and I have known each other since high school. There is nothing he isn't aware of about my eventful life. His love for me is the shower of blessing in my life. He is the pillar of my life.

He gently caressed me and said, "You are the strongest person I know. I have literally seen you flourish from the ground. We have gone through worst; this is nothing."

"Yeah…did she wake up again? Did she ask for me?" I asked.

"Yes…she woke up again. I told her that I let her go home to rest and that I'm there for her. She smiled and said she is feeling much better, but still a little drowsy. Then went back to sleep again," Albert said.

"That's when I decided to come home," he said.

I'm glad you are here; I said looking into his deep loving eyes. I'm lucky I have you. I kissed him gently on his lips. Albert always had a hard time resisting me. He is a well-controlled man. He can keep his emotions, wishes, desires for other aspects of life under the wraps if necessary, but for his emotions towards me. He gets vulnerable only with me. That was something I loved even more.

He held me tight and kissed me back. In no time, we got intense. He moved from my lips to my neck.

He stopped and asked, "Is Olga home?"

I said, "Yes, she will watch Ria."

He smiled sneakily and carried me to the bed and then quickly locked the bedroom door, and before I knew it, he was on top of me. We kissed for so long. Maybe because of the emotional night, the kiss turned out so intense. Albert enjoys the part when I call out his name while we were on it. And that day, I have no clue how many times I called out his name. His every touch, every kiss felt like the first time. I tried to keep my mourner quiet, but it was beyond my control. We cuddled for a long time until Ria knocked at the door. I quickly went to the bathroom to wear clothes while Albert opened the door.

Later that day, we went downstairs to meet Mother Catherine. She was fully awake by then but was in pain due to the surgery. She was happy to see us. She and Ria had the cutest conversation. I insisted Mother stay with us once she gets discharged from the hospital. She didn't refuse, so maybe, she would come to stay with us, I thought.

Albert is an architect. He had to get back to the office. So he left. I and Ria stayed with Mother for some more time. Then we let the mother take a rest and went to the gynecology department to visit my patient and the newborn. They were doing great. Ria was thrilled to see a tinier baby than her as she had thought she was the smallest. She insisted on carrying the baby, but I refused and let her touch and caress the baby instead. By the end of the day, I visited Dr. Samuel to check on Mother's condition; I was happy to know his diagnosis that she was stable and showing improvement. He said she can be discharged in three days' time if her improvement remains consistent.

The Past

Eleven

My life was going in a rut with burdening household work, Mom's responsibility, and my education. The days were literally flying as I was fighting-stop the battle of my life. But like a cactus in the middle of the desert, my love life was blossoming amongst all the havoc. Albert visited me every week. He brought notes and textbooks for me. I realized that he had an even bigger crush on me than I had on him. We both were too shy to express it. Every time he came, he would just give the books or talk about notes or class or school and leave. During these times, Jack grew into my best friend. He was nothing like his parents. He was friendly and kind-hearted. He didn't see me as an outsider who invaded their family. Instead, he treated me like family. Gradually, our trust bond became stronger. Jack too helped me with my studies. Jack knew about my soft spot for Albert, so when Albert came home, he would distract Aunty Laura and keep her busy so that we got some private moments.

There was no change in Aunty Laura's attitude towards me. In fact, it was getting worse day by day. She tried her level best to break me. But little does she know that I'm born strong and that strength and willpower are my twin souls. As long as Mom has a chance to get better and get back into her normal lifestyle, I am going to stay here and fight for her. It was hard but not impossible to fight against Aunty Laura. But Uncle Paul's obnoxious behavior and unpleasant looks were unbearably difficult to deal with. They had planned on giving my room to Jack and shifting me to the living room. But Jack refused to take it. Locking my room, the door was the only security I had at night. Every night I see someone trying to open my door knob from outside, and I had no doubt it was Uncle Paul. At first, I thought of involving Mother Catherine or social welfare in this. But I didn't have any proof against him, trying to get dirty with me. He cleverly stays on his best behavior when he is around others. His barbaric behavior plunges out only when he is alone with me. No one would even believe me if I said anything. I had a sense Jack was aware of his dad's devilish side. I decided to keep my eyes and ears open all the time, and if things start getting out of hand, I will get help from somewhere.

Every night, I sat next to Mom on her bed and told her about my day. I wasn't sure if she could hear me or understand what I was saying, but I got a sense of relief when I talked to her. Subconsciously, I was pretty sure that she could hear me. Until now, I haven't received any reaction from her. Not even a blink. She lay as if asleep. One day, I was sitting next to her as usual and chatting when Uncle Paul walked into the room.

He came in with his sneaky annoying smile and said, "What is my Barbie doll doing with her Mom!"

I ignored him completely and told Mom that I will see her later. As I was just about to get up from the bed, he sat next to me and stared intensely at me. There was anger and a feisty look in his eyes. I was trembling from inside but didn't want him to see my fear.

He angrily murmured, "Don't you dare ignore me. You both are living under our mercy in this house. So you better through that attitude of yours outside the window and obey what I say."

I replied crisply, "This is my parents' home, and I'm their daughter. And you are the unwelcome guests of our house who are shamelessly living in my parents' expenses. So technically, you are living under our mercy."

My reply invoked the beast inside him. Before I knew it, his hand was on my thigh. With his other hand, he lifted my skirt, and his hand had reached my private area. He pinched and squeezed it so hard that I cried out of pain. When I tried to move, he forced himself on me, and I lay on the bed helpless and unable to move while his one hand still hurt my sensitive part. I screamed and cried. His face was just a few inches apart from mine.

He ferociously said, "Who is in who's mercy now, HUH!"

I could smell the chicken we had for dinner in her breath. He was coming closer to my face when we felt a jerk on the bed. We turned around to see Mom looking straight into Uncle Paul's eyes furiously while hitting the bed with one hand as if she was trying to pierce a nail into the mattress with a hammer. In eleven months, this was the first time Mom had shown any sign of movement or reaction. It might have been Mom's eyes piercing right into his soul; he abruptly released me and stood up. He had shame, embarrassment, or terror on his face. And at the same moment, Jack forcefully pushed open the door as he had heard my scream.

Jack said curiously, "Jenny What's wrong? What happened?"

Jack stood there in shock when he saw Mom's vigorous movement and his dad standing terrified. He spontaneously knew something terrible has happened.

I tried to control Mom's reaction, but she didn't stop. She continued staring at Uncle Paul and hitting the bed. I called Mom's doctor. He came home and gave Mom an injection which soothed and let her go back to sleep.

The doctor said, "Something emotionally has triggered your mom to react. Even though it was a vigorous reaction, it's a positive step to the treatment. This is an indication that she could get better at any time. This is an indication of a speedy recovery."

Uncle Paul and Aunty Laura were not happy to hear that. I thought, "Though it was an abusive and brutish incident, something good came out of it."

I couldn't go back to sleep that night. It was painful, and I could still feel his hands and dirty touch in me, which made me feel physically and mentally contaminated. That traumatic experience provoked fear in me to live in that house. I was apprehensive about my safety and Mom's health. I decided that it's time to do something. "I should make a plan," I thought to myself. I saw the expression on their face when the doctor said Mom's reaction was a positive sign. It didn't look like that was something they were expecting to hear. I don't want them to do anything to sabotage my mom's advancement. I need solid proof to kick them out of my house. If I could get something in recording, that would be the best. Some flashes of ideas kept popping in my head. Finally, I decided to fix one of those baby cameras in my room, which some parents use to keep an eye on the nannies.

"I could probably get one of those from the security companies!" I thought.

But how do I get out of the house! And it might cost a lot! How do I fix it! My thoughts kept wandering over and again to the heinous incident and then again back to the camera like a pendulum of a clock. I didn't sleep even for minutes that night.

The next morning, I looked like hell with red swollen eyes and a dead look. Face drained out hair looked as if they were stuck in a tornado. When I was preparing breakfast, Jack came close to me and said, "Wow, you look like those hippy rockstars who haven't taken a shower in months."

He was trying to be funny and bring a smile to my face. But I was in no mood for humor. I smiled vaguely.

Jack said in a serious tone, "Jenny! I know something terrible happened in your mom's room yesterday, which impacted her to react. Even though her reaction was a positive sign, I know the incident wasn't pleasant. I just want you to know that if you feel like talking about it, I'm here. Or if you are planning on taking an action against it also, I'm with you. He is my father, but I don't support his nasty behaviors of his. He has a dirty mind. I will help you with anything you want to keep yourself away from him."

Jack's words floated like the poetry of relief into my ears. At least, there is one person in this house who supports me.

I told him, "I have a plan, and I might need your help. Can you please get Albert to come home in the evening today? I will share my idea with both of you together."

The day dragged like a snail. I kept myself occupied with work. But I could help but notice that Aunty Laura and Uncle Paul looked worried and panicky the whole time. They were whispering in the corners of the house, looked like they were plotting something. Aunty Laura later told me that she had to get some things done, so she and Paul were stepping out. She also added that they might be late, so I didn't have to make lunch for them. I knew they were up to something. But then, I had my own plotting and planning to do, so I thought if these people weren't at home when Albert and Jack came from school, it would be easier for us to plan and execute.

Jack came home with Albert. Paul and Laura hadn't returned yet. I thought I got the perfect opportunity. I told them about the fixing of the baby camera in my room. Albert agreed to buy the camera. He said he hadn't used his pocket money yet, so he would spend it on the camera, and Jack promised to get it fixed in my room and installed on Albert's laptop. I promised Albert I would return back every penny he spends on this mission. He smiled and said, "Take your time. It will give me an excuse to keep meeting you."

"I would be happier if you would keep meeting me without an excuse too," I said, blushing.

"I think I better leave you two alone," said Jack and left the room.

"I didn't want to ask in front of him. What happened? Did Paul misbehave with you? Did they hurt you?" Albert asked.

I looked down and stood silently, striving hard to stop the tears from flowing. I turned red in just a few moments and started shaking all over.

Albert touched my shoulders and said, "It's OK…It's OK…we are fixing the camera to catch these buggers red-handed. Whatever they did to you, I will go to any extent to make sure they reap what they sowed."

I burst out in tears hearing Albert's words. He gently hugged me. He was taller than me, so automatically, I laid my head on his chest and hugged him back. For a couple of minutes, I felt safe and secured. Probably, that was the moment when my soul knew that he was the one. He lifted my chin up and wiped my tears. He placed a kiss on my forehead. Then he looked directly into my eyes. We stared at each other as if we were the only two people on earth, and the whole world had become stagnant. He leaned forward and pressed his lips against mine. When his soft lips touched mine, the time stopped, my heart pounded fast and loud in my chest, my knees got weaker and something fluttered in my stomach. But even when the rest of my body was intensely reacting, all I could focus on was his lips softly rubbing against mine. When he withdrew, I thought how addictively he invaded all my senses. I wanted to pull him back to me, but I was too shy.

Without having expressed anything in words about our feelings for each other, we slid into our next phase in the relationship, like skiing in the snow.

Aunty Laura and Uncle Paul came much later than they had said. They still looked tensed and intense. They said they finished dinner, so I cleaned up the kitchen and went to my room. I couldn't wait for the cameras to be fixed so that I would have something solid in my hand. The next day, Albert bought the camera and sent it along with Jack. Jack hid it in his school bag and told me secretly that he will fix it later in the evening. He studied the instructions mentioned in the camera and passed them on to me so that both of us will be able to fix it together. Right above my bed, I have a wall stand filled with stuffed toys. The toys Dad had bought me when I was younger. We decided to hide the camera in between the toys so that it will get a good view. That angle will cover the door and my bed. The camera was connected to the server in Albert's house since we couldn't set up a server in the house because of Laura and Paul. Albert could access the camera from his computer at his house. The trap was ready now; we had to wait for the prey to be caught. The bait in my plan was me.

That night, I didn't lock my door. I lay down on my bed under the blanket. I was wide awake, waiting for Uncle Paul to come. I was terrified and sweating under the blanket but didn't want to step back from the plan. I want to live peacefully, and I want to give Mom a secure life. I have to do this. I thought of all the scenarios of how it might happen and didn't realize when I fell asleep. When I woke up, it was already morning, and my door was shut just like the way I had left it. "He didn't come last night," I thought. So whatever was going on with them was quite serious. I carried on the same plan the next night too, but he didn't come. I started wondering why he wasn't trying to open the door! The days and nights passed by without any action. Then on the sixth night, just like some days before, my door knob turned in the middle of the night. And there he was, standing like a huge monster. He was shocked to note that the door was unlocked. I was watching him from under the blanket. Rage was flowing through like lava under my skin, but I had to keep my calm at least till he attacked. He sneaked into the room and shut the door behind, and tried to lock it. But it wouldn't lock. Jack and I had removed the screws so that I wouldn't lock. He didn't mind that all the vulture could see was his prey lying there helplessly, and this was his moment to have her. He touched my legs with his big hairy arm. I think he was making sure I was under the blanket. He then forcefully pulled out my blanket and jumped on me. I could barely breathe with this heavy man lying on top with all his weight plunged on me. Before I could react, he started kissing me and pressing my breasts violently; I screamed and cried my lungs out so that Jack could hear me. Jack barged into the room and switched on all the lights. My scream woke Aunty Laura too. Laura was in shock. She shouted at her husband and asked him to leave the room. She then turned and threatened me not to say a word about this to a single soul. Or else she would put Mom and me in trouble.

Jack asked, "I hope our plan worked. When I get a chance, I will call Albert and ask if he got the recording. But, are you feeling OK Jenny?"

"It was painful and traumatic, but it would all be worth it if we got the recording," I replied.

I have always wondered how such a tender-hearted, caring, and loving boy was born to ruthless, selfish greedy people. He is literally the gem found in dirt.

Early during dawn, I was woken by a knock at the door. I opened the door and found Jack standing there grinning.

"We have it…we have it…" he said. I sighed in relief.

"My efforts are going to be rewarded," I thought.

I turned to Jack and asked, "You know what will happen once we hand over it, right? Are you upset, or are you having any second thoughts?"

"No, never…Go ahead with the plan. He should be punished for his actions. I'm completely on your side in this," he replied firmly.

I was so proud of Jack.

I called Mother Catherine and the child welfare authority employee home. Albert gave us the USB in which the previous night's incident was recorded. I played it with them in front of Aunty Laura, Uncle Paul, and Jack.

Mother Catherine looked at me in dismay. I could hear fury roar through her mind for Uncle Paul. She gave an infuriated look to Paul and Laura. Paul and Laura stood there silently as they couldn't come up with any stories because I brought their true colors out with solid proof. The social welfare authority immediately informed the police. The police arrested Paul. And said that Aunty Laura will be removed or replaced from being my legal guardian. She will have no power over Dad and Mom's money. She has to return everything either to me once I complete 18 or to Mom as and when she gets back to normal. The police said that she should go back to her home and report every time when called. She silently agreed to everything, and the next day, they left. I was sad that Jack had to go along with his mom. I wanted him to stay and complete his school education. But Aunty Laura wouldn't agree to it, as she knew Jack's presence would give me happiness, and she could never ever see me happy.

Before leaving, Jack told me, " Jenny, you are an amalgam of boldness and empathy, which is a rare but precious weave. With this attitude, you can win all your battles of life and conquer the world. Don't ever change. Be the powerhouse; you are perpetual. Out of all the negativities happening around, you have the sense to pick one tiny bit of positivity in the situation and proceed to hang on to it. I have learned a lot from you. I am sorry you had to go through a lot because of my parents. But I want our friendship to be for life. Take care, Jenny. We will catch up often."

Twelve

For the first time after almost a year, I felt safe in my house. My home was 'Home Sweet Home' once again. I spent half the day in my room reading, writing, and studying. I found solace in my books. I didn't eat anything because I didn't want to enter the kitchen. Visited Mom from time to time and gave her medicines. Somehow looking at Mom, I felt she was sleeping peacefully too. There was silence in the house, but it was the silence of harmony.

The next day, the social welfare authority said they wanted to meet me and Mother Catherine. I planned the meeting in the house. She said that they are proceeding with the legal process of transferring the power of attorney from Laura to Mother Catherine. Once the legal process is done, Mother will have the authority over Dad and Mom's bank accounts and property. I said with certainty that I am completely on board with it. She said she will deal with the rest of the formalities and get back to us.

After the social worker left, Mother asked me what was my next step. I said that once we get the money, I would love to go back to school or take up some extra home classes and focus on my education. She agreed to it. As we were talking, someone rang the doorbell. When I opened it, I was pleasantly surprised to see Olga. We were pleased to meet after a year. We hugged each other and had tears of joy flowing. "Not every relation needs a label. There are some relationships built purely out of love, respect, and sincerity," I thought.

Olga said, "I have been inquiring about you and Ma'am with the neighbors. When they told me Mr. Paul got arrested and Ms. Laura left the house, I decided to visit. Ms. Laura had strictly prohibited me from coming to this house."

"How are you handling, baby? How is Ma'am?" she asked lovingly.

"If you are OK, then I would love to come back to work. Don't worry about my salary, for now, we can decide about that with time. I have worked for Sir and Ma'am for nearly 25 years, and when ma'am was going through the worst time of her life, I had to leave her. I was weighing down heavily on guilt, regret, and shame for leaving her during these tough times. I want to come back and serve her. She is like a sister to me. Please, let me work for you," she said, weeping humbly.

I hugged her tightly and said, "Olga! You can stay as long as you want. You are a part of our family. Things were not in my control all these months. I am sorry I couldn't do anything when they asked you to leave. I would love to have you around. And I'm dying to eat your delicious food."

We all laughed, then Olga went upstairs to meet Mom. I turned to Mother and said, "Mother, I feel good about things happening around."

Olga's return was the icing on the cake. Spontaneously, she took up the responsibility of the house and Mom, which gave me more time to concentrate on my studies. I relished Olga's cooking and enjoyed the serenity. Maybe it was my instinct, or maybe because I had been struggling for so many months, my heart wasn't ready to fully dive into the peace and harmony. It sensed a storm behind the calm. Then I thought to myself that I will face it when it comes.

The social worker visited again after two days. Mother Catherine was also present when she came. She said she had come with the bad news. She said Laura doesn't have any money. Laura said she has spent all the money on Mom's treatment. There is only some left in the bank, which she has agreed to give to Jennifer.

I said shockingly, "She is lying. My parents are rich. Mom's treatment was covered by her medical insurance; we haven't spent a dime on her treatment. Laura has stolen our money!"

The social worker said, "We know she is lying. But we need proof. We checked all her bank accounts and other credits to verify for any transactions happening in the near past but couldn't get anything. I have registered an official complaint of fraud on her. Let the police do their job. She must have transferred the money into a burner account which is untraceable for now but not forever."

She continued, "In the meantime, you hang in there tight. Continue Mom's treatment through insurance. This might take time to get sorted. You will have to figure out a way to meet your expenses yourself. We will extend our help too. We will work it out together. Don't worry, Jennifer; this is just a temporary win for Laura. She won't get away with it."

I spoke to Jack regarding this. And as per his information, it wasn't long ago since they took the money. Jack said when Mom showed improvement, Laura and Paul realized that Mom would get up any day and their right over Mom and

Dad's money would slip away from their hands. So they plotted this forgery. When Jack told this, I remembered the way Laura and Paul behaved the next day of Mom's movement. They were all panicky and worried. This is what they were plotting.

As per the social worker, justice will be served, but the time taken can't be predicted. As far as Mom's medical insurance is intact, her treatment won't be affected. I had to do something about house expenses and my school fees. I dropped the idea of going back to school, which came to my head for a fraction of a second when Olga returned. There is absolutely no way I could afford school fees. I will have to let Olga go; how will I pay her salary? My thoughts kept rambling over the mishap and the possible solutions for it. I was absentmindedly staring into space when Olga said, "Baby, I heard everything the social worker said, please don't worry about my salary. I came back because I love you both. I will wholeheartedly stay with you until you need me. You can pay me whenever you are able."

It was as if Olga was reading my thoughts. I had no words to describe my gratitude towards her. At least one hassle is cleared. I will figure out a way for household expenses. I decided to go for a walk to clear my head.

After wandering around aimlessly for a while, I sat down on the bench of a park where children were playing, some people were jogging and exercising, and some others walking their dogs. Watching people living their life in peace elicited an imaginary silhouette of their happy lives. Am I the only one struggling in the world? Am I the only one fighting to survive? I was wrangling with myself in anguish. Then

Mom's face surfaced in my head. I recollected a trip down memory lane when she was up and active and strongly took care of the family, house, and job. She lived a carefree, exuberant life. Due to some unfortunate event, her life took a complete turn, and she is now laying in bed helpless.

While at the park, I overheard two ladies talking about their children. One said, "My son is having a hard time following math. I'm unable to help him as I work two jobs. I don't know what to do."

The other lady said, "Why don't you look for a private tutor! Personal attention will make a difference."

"Yeah, you are right. I will check with my friends if they know of any tutors," said the First Lady.

The boy they were talking about looked like he might be in year five. I thought I could give him private lessons for math! That way I can earn some money. But how do I talk to those ladies? Will they think I'm a freak! Nonetheless, I have to give it a shot. I proceeded to the ladies and said, "Hello, my name is Jennifer. I overheard your conversation about hiring a private tutor for your son. I would like to teach him. I'm a good student myself and have high scores in my class. I can guarantee your son will improve with me."

"Oh, that's nice; have you tutored anyone before?" asked the boy's mom.

"No! But I'm confident I can," I replied convincingly.

However, the lady was convinced and impressed with my smartness. And it turned out that she lived in the same street as mine. So she agreed to send the boy to my place every evening for tuition. I thought it's a good start. Slowly, with word of mouth, I might get more kids, which will be financial help for us.

Connor became a regular visitor of our house. He was a cute boy below average in math. He was in desperate need of help. Within a month, he started showing improvement in his studies. His mom was happy. She visited me when she came to give the fees and expressed her happiness. She said a friend of hers wanted to send her daughter too for tuition. She wanted to know if I would be interested in taking in new children. I enthusiastically agreed.

She said, "That's great! I will ask my friend to meet you."

Connor's tuition fee was the first earning of my life. I stared at the money in my hand and felt proud. Within the next couple of months, I had ten children coming for tuitions. They were in different levels, but luckily, all came for math. I was struggling to pay complete attention to each one. The tuition timings got extended with the increase in the number of children. I was swamped with tuition and my studies. Though I earned a decent amount of money, it wasn't nearly enough to pay for my school fees. The money was used for household purposes. I got more inquiries for tuitions, but I didn't take up new children. I wanted to do justice to these children. With more children, I won't be able to concentrate on each one as much as they need.

I will soon be in my final year of school, and I wanted to attend the classes to get good results. Home learning would be extremely tough in the final year. I had the plan to prepare for the Medical College admission test too, which needed a coaching class to be attended. I was in a dilemma, thinking about how I would make money for my classes. My tuition fees were barely covering the household needs.

At night, I went to Mom's room. It was my daily ritual to sit with Mom for some time at night and talk to her about my day. When I entered the room, I saw Mom on the floor. I was startled by the scene. I ran and tried to help her up but couldn't. I called out for Olga, and we both together got Mom up on the bed.

I asked Mom, "Mom, what happened? How did you fall down? Are you alright?"

She didn't respond, but her eyes were open and blinking. She looked at me for the first time in a year. She looked, and she just kept looking at me. I could see her facial muscles quivering. Either she was trying to say something or smile. However, it was a good sign, I thought. But for safety's sake, I called up her doctor. Her doctor examined and said that she has tried to get up and lost balance and fallen. It's an excellent sign, the doctor said. The doctor also asked us to keep a close watch on Mom for further developments.

That incident worried me a bit. We had no clue for how long Mom had been on the floor. What if she tries to move again and accidentally hurt herself! She still has difficulty moving her lips or talking. She wouldn't be able to call anyone for help. That's when I decided to move Mom to the bedroom downstairs so that either I or Olga will always be around her all the time.

The next day with the help of the hospital staff, we shifted Mom downstairs. She doesn't sleep all the time now. She lay down with her eyes open and watched us. That night when I went up to my room to sleep, I felt lonely upstairs. I went to Mom's room downstairs and slept with her. I thought, "Olga sleeps in the maid room. I can share the room with Mom downstairs. We could probably rent out the upstairs. We could earn some money that way!" I told my tuition kids about my renting out plan, and soon the word spread. Since we lived in a nice neighborhood and a pretty decent community, it wasn't much difficult to get tenants. Many queries came and finally, I chose a couple who worked at a bank near our house. They moved in within a couple of days. The rent from them partially helped us with our problems.

Meanwhile, Mom started showing tremendous improvement. When we make her sit upright, she was able to balance herself in that position and sit for hours. The doctor had given her spongy stress balls to strengthen her arm muscles. She would sit and keep squeezing the ball, shifting from one hand to another. As it is said, positive energy brings positivity to life. The moment the cynical people left the house, the light of hopefulness entered.

What I earned from the tuitions and the tenants was insufficient to meet my school fees. So I decided to skip my last year of school. I decided to continue as a home learner. I knew it was going to be fiendishly difficult to study on my own without being able to attend any practice sessions. But I had the confidence to do it. Well, I didn't have a choice. So I settled with the idea that I will try my level best to exceed well in the final year on my own, and if I don't score the marks, I expect to then, I will repeat the year. At the same time, if I could make some adjustments in the expenses, I could attend the medical admission test, coaching classes. I shared all my concerns with Mom and finally asked her if I could join the coaching class; she blinked with a gentle vague, smile. Mom's approving gesture was so assuring that my self-confidence got ignited, and I had a sudden feeling that I could conquer the world with Mom beside me. I was drained and exhausted from taking the house responsibilities and decisions on my own. Mom's one blink gave me the strength of a lion.

That evening, after a long time, I visited the family. Due to Aunty Laura's restrictions, Karen had stopped coming home. I was excited to meet her after so long.

"Hi, Jenny baby How are you? Mother Catherine told me about everything that happened. I'm sorry that you had to go through all that, but at the same time, I'm glad that you kicked those monsters out of your house! Way to go, girl! You are the boldest person I've ever met." said Karen excitedly.

"Yeah, things are good now," I replied.

But Karen is Karen; she could always read my mind. She stood grumpily with her arms crossed and looked straight into my eyes without saying a word.

"What???" I asked.

"HMM…why don't you save us both sometime and blurt out whatever is bothering you, or do you want me to punch your tummy and get it out." she said playfully.

I narrated to her about the financial issues and how Laura has stolen all my parents' money.

"Don't worry; you have figured out a way to sort half your problems. I'm sure we will find some solution for the rest too. I will inquire with other teachers of my school if they knew of any part-time job availability," she said.

Karen had recently completed her teacher's training course and started working as a teaching assistant in one of the primary schools. I knew she would become an amazing teacher; after all, she was my first teacher as a kid. We spent the rest of the time talking about Albert and the line of boys Karen dated. With Karen, I didn't realize how fast time went by.

Thirteen

It has been almost five months since I joined the coaching class, and was busy with my school studies. It was quite challenging to learn on my own. Meanwhile, my tuition kids went up to 15. Even though I was going through a grueling schedule, there was a delightful fulfillment in life as I was following the path towards my goal.

Mom moved from the bed to a wheelchair. She still couldn't stand on her feet or walk. But her hand regained its strength, and she could wheel herself around the house. She started eating solid food herself. She began to talk, but the words were undefined. Olga and I could pick up what she tried to say.

One day, Karen came home. She wanted to pass on the contact information of one of her student's parents who was a nurse in a hospital in the city. Karen said she had spoken to the parent, and she said there was a part-time job opening in her hospital. I decided to give it a try. I contacted the nurse, and she guided me to visit the HR of the hospital. When I went to the hospital, it was brought to my notice that it was a receptionist job at the gynecology department for the night shift. I agreed to it immediately. I presumed since it's the night shift, my studies won't get disrupted, and my future goal was to become a gynecologist, so being around the doctors and nurses might help me in some way or the other.

I started my job from the following week onwards. Within a blink of time, my life became supremely busy. During the day, I attended my coaching class, the evenings were occupied by tutoring, and at 8 pm, my hospital duty started. I was working from 8-6. Once I'm back home, I would sleep for a couple of hours. My mind and days were engrossed with my own busy schedule that I didn't even think of Laura or the money. The tutoring fee, rent, and hospital salary combined led our life smoothly. I was even able to pay salary to Olga, notwithstanding the fact that she refused to take it every time. Once from the depth of her heart, Olga said that the best decision Mom and Dad had ever taken was to adopt me. She added that she was aware that Mom was proud of me. Although I had realized that a zillion times myself that I was unquestionably lucky to have been chosen by Mom and Dad. I'm sure my biological parents were neither happy nor proud of me; that's why they abandoned me.

Through the medium of my classmates and Albert, I could complete my final exam. My score was pretty decent, but as per my capability, I could have scored more. Anyway, I was happy to complete my schooling. In a month's time, I was going to give the medical college admission test. Since my school scores weren't that great, I had to give my lock, stock, and barrel on this test. Nonetheless, I was uncertain about the future education plan if I passed the admission test. But I decided to go with one step at a time. At that stage, my aim was to pass the admission test with flying colors. I concluded that baby steps will only take me forward. I put in all my energy and effort in studies for the next month. And when finally, the day of my test arrived, I was delusional. I was getting ready, but I felt my brain had deranged. I couldn't establish why I felt that way. While at the breakfast table, Olga said, "Why do you look lost? Don't think too much, baby. I've seen all the hard work you have put in for this test. I am convinced that you are going to get into medical college."

That's when it hit me. My heart and brain were in a battle, as my heart wanted me to get into the medical college while my brain questioned how will I proceed with it even if I passed!

I sat there motionless with my untouched breakfast in front of me. Mom came to me and held my hand, and smiled. That was exactly what I wanted to get going. I prepared so hard to pass the test, and what happens after that can be taken care of later. "I will give my hundred percent," I assured Mom.

I had heard from Mother Catherine that "when a person wholeheartedly put in all the effort to achieve a goal, the universe will provide the nudge in an unexpected form." We could call it an Angel or Godsend or blessing in disguise or answer to our prayers. That's how it works, and I personally experienced it. I passed my medical college admission test with high scores. And while I wondered how to go forward, our tenants, the bankers, who had seen all the hardship our family had gone through and the effort I had put in, helped me get a student loan from their bank under their own guarantee. It was a two-year loan. I promised them that once our case against Laura gets solved, I would repay them. With the few months of stay at our house, we built trust in each other. They said, "We feel fortunate in getting an opportunity to help a bright student fulfill her dream. Please concentrate on your studies and don't worry about repaying. We will consider it as goodwill if you cannot repay us."

They were genuinely Godsend!

I was officially an MBBS student. I was immensely proud to be called that. There were four years of a bachelor's degree and another three years to complete MD. When I started college, I didn't know how far I would be able to take it. But I wasn't the one to quit. I believed that the path will clear its way automatically along with the journey. My campus was in the same compound of the hospital where I was working as the receptionist, which made the transmute easier. It was extremely challenging with the night shift and day college and just three hours of sleep in between. My hectic schedule took a toll on my health, but I fought against all the odds. Concurrently, Mom's physiotherapy sessions determined its results. She started walking using crutches. Her vocal enunciation improved. I couldn't sustain myself with my tutoring anymore, so Mom took over. She was pleased to be proactive and helpful. Her confidence boosted as she was lending her contribution to the house.

One night, while I was on duty, I hadn't received any calls, nor were there any emergency cases. During those times, I used to study. Maybe I was exhausted due to my frenetic schedule; I dozed off on the table with my books open. That's when our senior gynecologist, Dr. Riya Augustine walked in. She knocked at my desk; I jumped from my seat, flipping my books. She went through my book and asked me to join her in her cabin. For an instant, I was petrified that she was going to fire me. I couldn't afford to lose my job. I walked behind her like a sneaky terrified kitten.

She was my idol. She was the most respected and experienced doctor in the hospital. I wanted to learn a lot from her. And here, I thought even before I got a chance, I will be fired. We went inside her cabin, and she gestured me to sit down.

Dr. Riya asked, "Are you a medical student?"

I stammered, "yyyess."

"Is this a part-time job you do?"

"Yyyeess…I'm sorry, Ma'am, I will be careful hereafter…I will make sure I don't fall asleep…" I blabbered.

She smiled and said, "It's OK, dear. I know how hard the studies can get. I'm just wondering how you are able to manage a night job and education. Why do you work here?"

I narrated my life to her without leaving out anything. She patiently listened to my whole story and said, "I'm really proud of you, Jennifer. From tomorrow onwards, I give you permission to tag along with me while I attend cases and surgeries. You will not touch a thing or give your suggestions or opinions to the patients. You can observe, understand and educate yourself. You can ask me any doubts you have. I will be happy to help. I like bright students, and I would love to see you become a successful gynecologist."

"But one thing I want to know, why are you so adamant in becoming a gynecologist? Why not any other profession?" she added.

I said, "Ma'am, whoever gave birth to me, abandoned me without any hesitation. I am blessed with a mother and father, but there are times when I wondered what my real parents looked like and what went through their minds when they decided to give up on me. I don't want any infant to have a fate like mine. I cannot protect the whole world, but by becoming a gynecologist, at least if the mother I'm helping to give birth doesn't want to keep the baby, I will take care of the baby, and I will not allow anyone to just abandon the baby like a piece of garbage."

Dr. Riya inferred my pain, frustration, bitterness, and resentment in that one sentence of mine. She said, "I cannot imagine what you went through, but I understand. I will guide you."

Dr. Riya became my mentor. I learned so much from her. She regularly visited some nearby villages to give free consultations and also counseled women throughout their pregnancy and delivering the baby. She conducted free seminars regarding the female reproductive system, pregnancy, and childbirth. She even did the procedure of childbirth with minimal technical equipment. And that was something I couldn't have learned from any college or books. Initially, I was merely tagging along taking notes and enlightening my knowledge, but gradually, she started delegating me with minor jobs like handing over the prescriptions, surgical instruments and printing the reports, etc. I was turning into her right hand.

Meanwhile, our case against Laura ended, and she had to return all our money. Although she had spent a lot of it, we were happy at least we got half of it back. Laura was sent to jail for forgery. Jack was alone. He had joined a college near his home. I insisted him to come and live with us. But he refused saying that staying in his own home will be more convenient for him to attend college. However, he joined us during the weekends.

After receiving the money, Mom and I repaid our tenants their money in installments. They loved staying in our home, so we let them extend their contract. In a way that gave us more time to pay back the loan too.

The Present

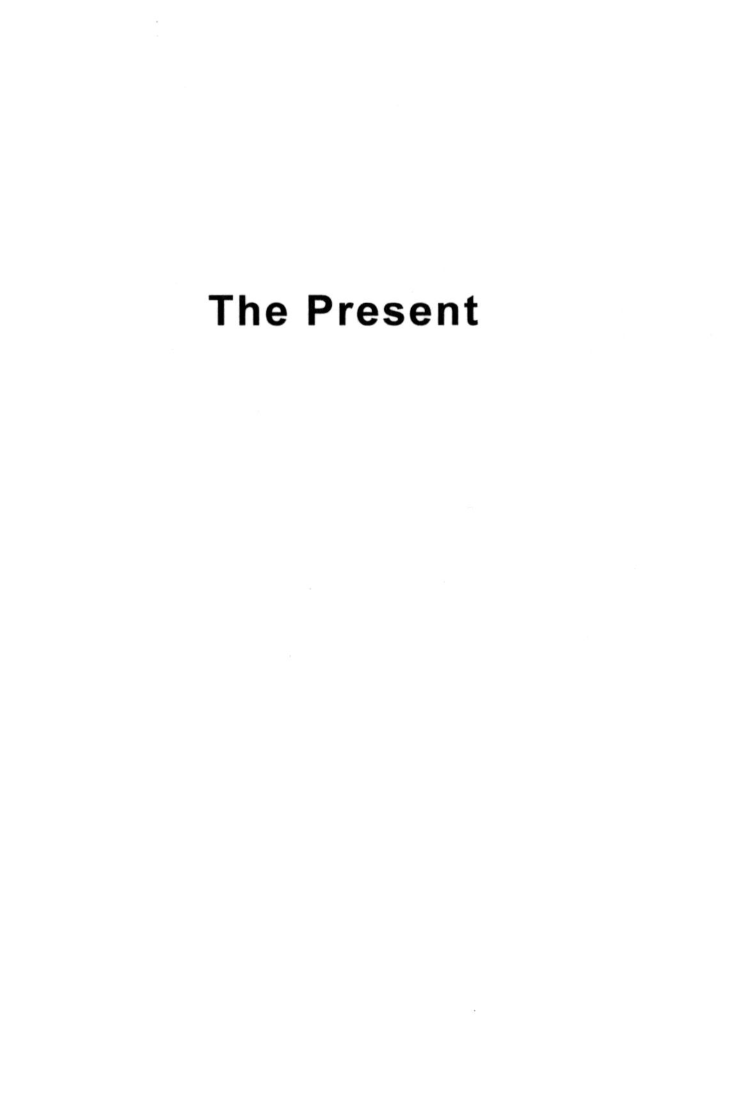

Fourteen

Karen screamed from the kitchen, "I hope Mother is allowed to have chicken soup and salad."

"Why are you screaming? I'm right here," I replied from the kitchen storeroom.

"Ohh! I didn't know you were here," she said, and we laughed out loud.

"What are you girls doing?" asked Mom walking into the kitchen.

"Nothing, Mom, it's just Karen being her silly self," I said, rolling my eyes.

"Granny! Granny! Come play with us," said Ria and Caleb.

"Mommy, can I have cookies with Ria?" asked Caleb to Karen.

Karen replied, "Yes dear, today is a happy day. You can have anything you want."

So can I have ten cookies?

"No! Just two," she said, giggling.

The kids pulled Mom out of the kitchen. I heard Albert saying loudly from the living room, "Come on kids, don't drag granny like that. She cannot run like you both."

For which Mom replied playfully, "Ahem ahem…Yes, she can! She has spent a long time lying powerlessly in bed. Not anymore. Granny is the happiest person on earth now, and she wants to run and jump and play with my adorable grandkids."

Karen came out of the kitchen and said to her husband, who was sitting on the couch with Albert enjoying a drink, "Pete, Olga is on the way. She will take care of the rest of the arrangements in the kitchen. Jenny and I are going downstairs to bring mother home. You guys make sure kids don't get too naughty with Mom."

Pete replied, "Don't worry, we will take care of the things here. You both go and make necessary arrangements for Mother's discharge."

Albert added whimsically, "Don't ruin the surprise out of excitement. Remember we all have gathered here to surprise Mother."

"We know!" we both said at the same time.

Karen and I went to the hospital to bring Mother home. There were some usual procedures of discharge, which took about 45 minutes to be completed. We brought her upstairs in a wheelchair as she wasn't yet good enough to walk. She was delighted to see both of us together. She started inquiring about our kids and life in general. It was tough to reserve our contentment, but we both did a fair job.

When we reached outside my apartment door, I took out the key from my pocket as if we were the only ones in the house. I had called Albert before arriving to indicate to him that we were on the way. I opened the door, and the moment we rolled Mother inside, everyone screamed, "SURPRISE!" Mother hadn't expected to see everyone together. She was overwhelmed with the warmth and love. She had tears rolling down her cheeks. She hugged Ria and Caleb. She was thrilled to see Albert and Pete. And there was a few moments of an emotional hug between Mom and Mother Catherine. We shared pleasantries for a little while and then decided to have lunch. It was a full house on the dining table, but we arranged some extra chairs so that all of us could sit together. Once we all sat down, I called Olga. She refused and said she will eat later. But I said she was a part of our family and that she has to have lunch with us on this special day. Suddenly Albert said, "Oh wait, I promised I would call someone." And he went to the bedroom and came back with his laptop. He placed his laptop next to the dining table. Albert face-timed Jack, who was living in a different country now. It was the most beautiful day of our lives. None of us were related by blood to each other, but we were a big happy family. My family.